餐旅英文與會話
Practical Hotel, Restaurant, and Travel English

謝雯雯 / 著

褚序

　　有句話說「觀其友而知其人」，若將這樣的話，套用在出版界的話，那麼應該就是「觀其人而知其書」了。作者謝雯雯，是我教導的學生中最傑出的其中一位，在她求學的過程裡，讓我深深感受到她對每件事認真與執著的態度。兩年前，得知她受出版社的器重，正要開始著手出版一本有關餐旅飯店的英文書，非常為她感到高興，因為我知道，從她求學積極、認真且謹慎的態度，就可以預期，她一定會傾全力，將這本書做到盡善盡美，務實好用。

　　果不其然，這本書在她辛苦默默耕耘之下，誕生了。雖然是初試啼聲之作，但是內容與編排，絕對屬出版界中上乘之作。市面上有許多類似餐飲飯店管理的書，但許多都流於刻板過時，像這種屬於生活應用的英語工具書，取材的新穎與否，攸關一本書的成敗。在這個部分，作者可說是蒐集了目前最新最普遍而且最好用易記的語料，並不時地透過相關最新資訊，做求證與更新。很榮幸能在自己學生的著作當中，盡一分綿薄之力，在這過程之中，讓我對這位傑出的學生更加肯定，也對這本書深具信心。

　　觀其友而知其人，觀其人而知其書。作者謹慎務實的處事風格，

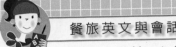
完全映證在她這本著作當中，相信這本書必定能讓您感受到作者的用
心與認眞的態度，會是一本讓你覺得實用充實，獲益良多的好書。

武陵高中　褚謙吉老師　May, 2010

序

　　《餐旅英文與會話》主要針對餐廳、旅館、旅遊等主題設計而成。本書適用的對象，除了一般大專院校的餐飲科學生、高中職餐飲科學生以及常出國旅遊的一般民眾，或是對於應用英文，特別是餐旅英文有興趣的讀者，皆能以此書入門。

　　本書的特色包括：

1. 本書以表格及圖像幫助學習及記憶，提綱挈領，一目了然。

2. 筆者特別設計「大哉問」單元，以讀者的角度提問，增進讀者思考以及理解。

3. 章末延伸學習，可增加學習的廣度，厚植實力。

4. 針對不同情境設計實境對話，在日常生活或是出國旅遊當中皆可應用，並隨書附上朗讀CD，方便讀者模仿及練習發音及語調。

5. 每節後有小試身手、每章後有實戰演練試題可供讀者做複習，並找出學習的缺失。

　　建議讀者可以參考以下方法，充分使用本書，提升自己的能力：

1. 熟記單字，以本書所附之圖片幫助記憶，如場景圖（餐廳、飯店、機場）。

2. 熟記常用表達法，特別是要針對不同情境做適當的問答。

3. 可搭配CD，熟練對話，特別注意上下文，社交禮儀，以及如何應對。

4. 勤做題目，更加熟練。

5. 熟記關鍵語句，如 "May I help you?"，"How would you like to pay?"，"May I take the order?"，"Did you make a reservation?" 等等。

6. 有問題勇於發問及討論。

7. 找同學或是朋友做角色扮演，模擬各種情境，進行英文會話的演練。

8. 若日常生活或是與家人朋友出國旅遊時，別忘了學以致用喔！

　　最後筆者要感謝許多人，褚謙吉老師義不容辭，幫忙審稿，陳盈潔老師鼓勵我接下這本書的執筆工作，以及美國的朋友Stephanie Fann在對話編寫上，給我很多建議，另外，還要謝謝我的家人在這段期間給我的支持。

謝雯雯　May, 2010

如何使用本書

　　本書共有十四個主題，每一個主題包含：

1.學習重點（Introduction）

　　預知本書重點，並引導讀者學習的方向。

2.常用字彙（Useful Words）

　　在每個主題一開始，整理各主題重要單字，方便讀者預習此一主題常用的單字。

3.常用的表達方法（Useful Expressions）

　　提供主題各種情境下實用的句型。

4.會話（Conversation）

　　設計各種情境會話，讓讀者實戰演練。

5.重要單字片語（Word Bank）

　　整理每個會話重要的單字和片語。

6.小試身手（Quiz）

　　讀者可快速測驗一下自己吸收的程度。

7.延伸學習（Extension）

　　增加學習的廣度及深度，基礎穩固之後，更上一層樓。

8.單一選擇題（Multiple Choice）

針對不同的主題，檢驗學習成效。

另外，並設計大哉問此一專欄，解答讀者可能提出來的問題。

目録

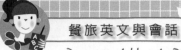

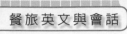

Talking about Time
1 時間的說明

 本章摘要

Units of Time 時、分、秒的說法

What Time Is It? 時間的說明

What Date Is Today? 年、月、日、星期的說明

Extension 延伸學習

Introduction 學習重點

　　時間觀念是現代人非常重視的禮貌，尤其在帶團或是跟團等團體行動時，每個人對於守時重視程度，將會大大影響了旅遊的品質。學會時間的說法及表示方法，是理解及溝通時間的基礎。時間的重要性，在日常生活中，也是隨處可見。例如出發時間、回程時間、集合時間、表演時間、開車時間、吃飯時間、晨喚時間等等不勝枚舉。我們主要用年（years）、月（months）、週（weeks）、日（days）、小時（hours）、分（minutes）、秒（seconds）來測量及指稱時間。

Useful Words 常用字彙

1000 milliseconds	=1 second
60 seconds	=1 minute
60 minutes	=1 hour
24 hours	=1 day
7 days	=1 week
28, 29, 30 or 31 days	=1 month
365 or 366 days	=1 year
12 months	=1 year
10 years	=1 decade
100 years	=1 century
1000 years	=1 millennium

Units of Time 時、分、秒的說法

Useful Expressions 常用的表達方法

時間單位

second 秒	There are sixty seconds in one minute.
minute 分	There are sixty minutes in one hour.
hour 時	There are twenty-four hours in one day.

時間的表達法

a little/short while 一會兒	A: How much longer are we going to stay at the museum? B: We're going to stay here for **a little while**, I think. A: 我們還要留在博物館裡多久？ B: 還要一會兒，我想。
a moment 一段很短的時間	A: Could you wait **a moment**, please? B: I'm in a hurry, so it has to be quick. A: 能請你稍等一下嗎？ B: 我在趕時間，所以快一點。
a minute（大約一分鐘上下的時間）	A: When are you going to leave here? B: In just **a minute**. A: 你何時要離開？ B: 一分鐘內。
a few seconds 幾秒鐘（一段很短的時間）	A: Are you done with your work? B: No, but it'll be done in a few seconds. A: 你做完工作了嗎？ B: 還沒，但很快就會完成了。

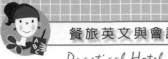
How many seconds/minutes/hours does/did it take 人 to V...？ …花了某人幾秒／分鐘／小時？	How many minutes does it take you to walk from the hotel to the nearest convenience store? 從飯店走到最近的便利商店，需要花你幾分鐘？
How much time do/does/did 人 spend +V-ing...? 某人花了多少時間做某事？	How much time do we spend eating breakfast? 我們花了多少時間吃早餐？
How long do/does/did 人 spend +V-ing...? 某人花了多長的時間做某事？	How long did you spend taking a shower? 你淋浴淋了多久？

Conversation 會話

(*A hotel guest is talking to a desk clerk.*)

Clerk: Good morning. May I help you?

Guest: Yes. Could you please **direct** me to the swimming pool?

Clerk: It's on the eighth floor.

Guest: Thanks. **By the way**, when does it open?

Clerk: In about a **half** hour. Do you have any other questions?

Guest: Oh, yes! Does this hotel have a **shuttle bus** to **Disneyland**?

Clerk: We do have a shuttle to Disneyland. **However**, I need to **check** when it leaves. Please wait here for a short while. I will give you a **correct schedule** in a few moments.

Guest: That's okay. **Take your time**.

(*After the guest waits about two minutes...*)

Clerk: The next one will leave in ten minutes. Here is the schedule.

Guest: How much time does it take to get to Disneyland from here?

Clerk: It will take you about forty minutes.

（飯店的客人正在跟櫃檯人員說話）
櫃檯人員：早安。有什麼可以為你服務的地方嗎？

客人：嗯，可以請你告訴我游泳池怎麼去嗎？

櫃檯人員：游泳池在八樓。

顧客：謝謝。對了，它什麼時候會開放？

櫃檯人員：大約再一個小時過後。你還有其他問題嗎？

顧客：嗯，有！這家飯店有前往迪士尼樂園的接駁車嗎？

櫃檯人員：我們有提供接駁車。但是，我還需要確認一下發車時間。
請在這裡等我一下。幾分鐘後，我會給你正確的時刻表。

顧客：沒關係。慢慢來。

（約兩分鐘過後……）

櫃檯人員：下一班車十分鐘後會出發。這是時刻表。

顧客：從這裡到迪士尼樂園要花多少時間？

櫃檯人員：大約需要四十分鐘的時間。

Word Bank 重要單字片語

1. direct [dəˋrɛkt] v. 給…指路

2. By the way 順便問一下

3. half [hæf] adj. 一半；二分之一

4. shuttle bus [ˋʃʌtḷ bʌs] n. phr. 接駁車

5. Disneyland [ˋdɪznɪlˌlænd] n. 迪士尼樂園

6. however [hauˋɛvɚ] adv. 然而

7. check [tʃɛk] v. 確認,檢查

8. correct [kəˋrɛkt] adj. 正確的

9. schedule [skˋɛdʒul] n. 時刻表；日程安排表

10. Take your time 慢慢來

Quiz 小試身手：請寫出正確英文單字

1. Q: How m_____ time does it t_____ to walk from our hotel to the nearest supermarket?

   A: About f_____ m_____(=a quarter).

2. How l_____ did you s_____ having dinner tonight?

答案：much, take, fifteen, minutes, long, spend

What Time Is It? 時間的說明

Useful Expressions 常用的表達方法

現在幾點？

Formal （正式說法）	Do you have the time? Have you got the time? May I have the time, please?
Informal （非正式說法）	What's the time? What time is it?

回答的方式

1.The time is...

2. It's...（較常使用）

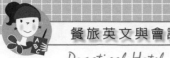
範例：

Question	What's the time, please?
Answer	It's five o'clock.

以下有兩種方式，來說明時間。其中要注意幾個字：

1. past：經過，也可用after表示。e.g. ten past three 三點過了十分鐘

2. to：還差（幾分鐘）。e.g. three minutes to ten 還差三分鐘十點

3. (a) half 一半：e.g. half an hour=30 minutes

4. a quarter：15 minutes

	It's...(informal) 分+時	It is...(formal) 時+分
3:00	three o'clock	three
3:02	just gone three o'clock	three oh two
3:03	three minutes past three	three oh three
3:05	five past three	three oh five
3:09	nine minutes past three	three oh nine
3:10	ten past three	three ten
3:15	a quarter past three	three fifteen
3:20	twenty past three	three twenty
3:21	twenty-one minutes past three	three twenty-one
3:25	twenty-five past three	three twenty-five
3:30	half past three	three thirty
3:35	twenty-five to four	three thirty-five
3:40	twenty to four	three forty
3:45	a quarter to four	three forty-five

3:50	ten to four	three fifty
3:55	five to four	three fifty-five
3:57	three minutes to four	three fifty-seven
3:58	nearly four o'clock	three fifty-eight
4:00	four o'clock	four

Conversation 會話

(*A hotel guest is talking to a desk clerk.*)

Guest: Is there a shuttle bus from the hotel to the **airport**?

Clerk: Yes, ma'am. The first shuttle bus will **leave** in fifteen minutes, at eight fifty a.m.

Guest: When will the next one leave?

Clerk: It leaves every thirty minutes.

Guest: What time does your **restaurant** open?

Clerk: It opens at eight a.m.

Guest: Thank you!

Clerk: You're welcome.

（一位飯店裡顧客正在跟櫃檯服務人員談話。）

顧客：請問有沒有從飯店到機場的接駁車？

櫃檯人員：有的，女士。第一班接駁公車將會在十五分鐘後，也就是
　　　　　八點五十分發車。

顧客：下一班車是什麼時候？

櫃檯人員：每三十分鐘一班。

客人：你們的餐廳幾點開始營業？

櫃檯人員：早上八點。

客人：謝謝。

櫃檯人員：不客氣。

Word Bank 重要單字片語

1. airport [`ɛr,pɔrt] n. 機場

2. leave [liv] v. 離開

3. restaurant [`rɛstə,rant] n. 餐廳

Quiz 小試身手：請寫出正確英文單字

1. Q: M_____ I h_____ the time, please?（正式用法）

A: It's three ten (= ten _____ _____).

2. Q: When will you arrive here?

A: At _____ fifty (= _____ _____ four).

答案：May, have, past, three, three, ten, to

What Date Is Today? 年、月、日、星期的說明

Useful Expression 常用的表達方法

星期幾

	Day 星期	Abbreviation 縮寫	
weekdays 週間	Monday	Mon.	Mo.
	Tuesday	Tue.	Tu.
	Wednesday	Wed.	We.
	Thursday	Thu.	Th.
	Friday	Fri.	Fr.
weekend 週末	Saturday	Sat.	Sa.
	Sunday	Sun.	Su.

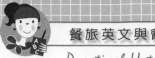
月分

以下依照月分的順序排列。並列出月分、月分縮寫、一個月有幾天以及季節。

其中季節只是大約，因為季節分布跟緯度有關，以下是根據如北美洲等地的季節分布為例，在南半球季節分布則相反。

	Month 月分	Short Form 簡寫	Days 天數	Season 季節
1	January	Jan.	31	Winter
2	February	Feb.	28/29	
3	March	Mar.	31	Spring
4	April	Apr.	30	
5	May	May	31	
6	June	Jun.	30	Summer
7	July	Jul.	31	
8	August	Aug.	31	
9	September	Sep.	30	Autumn
10	October	Oct.	31	
11	November	Nov.	30	
12	December	Dec.	31	Winter

日 期

1st	first
2nd	second
3rd	third
4th	fourth
5th	fifth
6th	sixth
7th	seventh
8th	eighth
9th	ninth
10th	tenth
11th	eleventh
12th	twelfth
13th	thirteenth
14th	fourteenth
15th	fifteenth
16th	sixteenth
17th	seventeenth
18th	eighteenth
19th	nineteenth
20th	twentieth

21st	twenty-first
22nd	twenty-second
23rd	twenty-third
24th	twenty-fourth
25th	twenty-fifth
26th	twenty-sixth
27th	twenty-seventh
28th	twenty-eighth
29th	twenty-ninth
30th	thirtieth
31st	thirty-first

1. Q: What day is today? 今天星期幾？

   A: It's _____. (Monday, Tuesday...)

2. Q: What date is today? 今天是幾月幾號？

   A: It's _____. (July first, May twenty-fifth...)

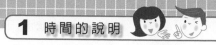

Conversation 會話

(*A visitor is talking to a clerk at the* ***information desk*** *in a* ***museum***.)

Visitor: **Excuse me**. Is the museum open seven days a week?

Clerk: No, ma'am. It's **closed** on Tuesday.

Visitor: This museum looks very old. When was it built?

Clerk: Yes, it was **built** in 1789 and is a historic landmark.

Visitor: Wow, it's been a long time and is still in great **shape**. When
do you close today?

Clerk: We're open nine hours a day, from eight thirty to five thirty.

Visitor: By the way, what day is today?

Clerk: It's Thursday.

Visitor: I'm sorry, I mean, what's today's date ?

Clerk: It's June 6th.

Visitor: Can I **reserve** a **group** visit for this Saturday?

Clerk: Sure, **hold on a minute, please.** I'm sorry. We're closed for a **private** party on this Saturday. What about June 15th, next Saturday?

Visitor: Yes, that will be fine.

Clerk: Okay. So I will make you a reservation for a group visit on Saturday, June 15th

（博物館裡，有一位遊客正和詢問處的服務人員談話。）

遊客：不好意思，請問這間博物館每天都會開放嗎？

服務人員：不，女士。星期二公休。

遊客：這間博物館看起來歷史悠久。這是什麼時候建造的？

服務人員：沒錯，它興建於1789年。它是一座歷史古蹟。

遊客：哇，的確歷史悠久而且外表看起來維護得很好。今天開放到幾點?

服務人員：從上午八點半至下午五點半，一天開放九個小時。

遊客：對了，今天的日期是？

服務人員：今天是星期四。

遊客：抱歉，我的意思是……今天是幾月幾日？

服務人員：6月6日。

遊客：我可以預約這星期六的團體參觀嗎？

服務人員：當然可以，請稍等一下。很抱歉，由於私人團體活動的關
係，這星期六不會開放。那下星期六，6月15日呢？

遊客：好的。

服務人員：沒問題。那麼我會替你預約6月15日，星期六的團體參觀。

Word Bank 重要單字片語

1. information desk [͵ɪnfɚ`me ʃən dɛsk] n. phr. 詢問處；服務台

2. museum [mju`ziəm] n. 博物館

3. Excuse me. 不好意思（通常是有所請求時說）

4. closed [klozd]（close的過去分詞 v. 關閉）

5. built [bɪlt]（build的過去分詞，建造）

6. shape [ʃep] n.形狀；情況；狀態

7. reserve [rɪ`zɝv] v. 預訂

8. group [grup] n. 群；團體

9. Hold on a minute, please. 請稍待片刻

10. private [`praɪvət] adj. 私人的

Quiz 小試身手：請寫出正確英文單字

1. Q: What _____ is today? A: It's Saturday.

2. How _____ do you take a trip? A: _____ a year. （一年兩次）

答案：day, often, twice

Extension 延伸學習：其他時間的表達方法

at 跟 in 的差別在哪？

at： 後接特定的時間 e.g. at two thirty p.m.

in：有三個意思

1. 在…期間(during): It's six o'clock in the afternoon.

2. 在…之後(before or at the end of)：The bus will leave in five minutes.

3. 在…之內(within)：In ten minutes, he ate three hamburgers.

on 跟 in 的差別在哪？

on： 後接星期特定的時間 e.g. It's on Monday.

in：後接月分跟年分

e.g.

1. I will be there in October.

2. The park was built in 2002.

那我們一般看到 A.M. 或 P.M. 是指什麼？

1. A.M. (Ante-Meridiem = before noon) 從午夜十二點之後開始算。

   e.g. 7:30 a.m.

   seven thirty a.m.(formal)　　seven thirty in the morning (informal)

2. P.M. (Post-Meridiem=after noon) 從中午十二點之後開始算。

   e.g. 7:30 p.m.

   seven thirty p.m.(formal)　　seven thirty in the evening (informal)

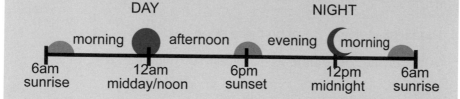

那「閏年」的英文要怎麼說？

每四年會有一次二月會有29天，這一年叫做閏年，這一年就叫 "leap year"，因此，這一年有366天。2月29日（29th February）這一天就叫 "leap day"。

How long / soon / often 有什麼不同？

How long...? …多久？	How long have you lived in Taipei? 你住台北多久了？
How soon? …多快？	How soon can you finish your homework? 你多快可以完成你的回家作業？
How often...? …多常？	How often do you play basketball? 你多常打籃球？

Multiple Choice 單一選擇題

1. A _____ is about 12 months.
   (A) year (B) month (C) week (D) day

2. A _____ of an hour is 15 minutes.
   (A) half (B) midnight (C) quarter (D) double

3. There are 60 _____ in an hour.
   (A) seconds (B) moments (C) hours (D) minutes

4. Please wait a _____. I'll be there soon.
   (A) weekend (B) moment   (C) year (D) minutes

5._____ comes after Thursday.
   (A) Sunday (B) Monday (C) Friday (D) Tuesday

6. _____ is the second month of the year.
   (A) March (B) February (C) January (D) November

7. The museum opens from Tuesday to _____.
   (A) 6 p.m. (B) December 30th (C) Friday (D) ten days

8. A: _____

   B: It's Thursday.

   (A) What day is today? (B) What's the weather like?

   (C) What is the date today? (D) What's your name?

9. A: What is the date today?

   B: _____

(A) It's December first. (B) It's October. (C) It's a holiday.

(D) It's hot and humid.

10. A: What time is the shuttle bus?

    B: _____

    (A) On Friday. (B) Every day. (C) 9 a.m. (D) On June first.

11. A: Do you have the time?

    B: _____

    (A) Yes. It's a lovely day.

    (B) No. I think it's eight p.m.

    (C) No. She is not on time.

    (D) Yes. It's eight twenty-five.

12. A: Excuse me, _____?

    B: It's a quarter past ten.

    (A) do you have times (B) may I have the time

    (C) what date is today (D) may I help you

13. A: _____

    B: I've been in Taipei for five years.

    (A) Have you ever been to Taipei?

    (B) When will you go to Taipei?

    (C) How long have you been in Taipei?

    (D) Did you enjoy your dinner?

14. A: I want to take the MRT to Taipei Main Station. _____

   B: Every four minutes.

   (A) When does the next train arrive?

   (B) How often does it run?

   (C) When will I get there?

   (D) Where can I buy the ticket?

15. A: Does the bus run on time?

   B: _____

   (A) No. It may be ten minutes late.

   (B) Yes. There will be no bus after 11 p.m.

   (C) Yes. It goes to the hotel.

   (D) It's late again.

16. A: When does it open?

   B: _____.

   (A) Yes. It opens at 8 a.m.

   (B) In 1986.

   (C) In about an hour.

   (D) Two days.

17. A:_____ do you go shopping?

   B: Once a month.

   (A) How soon

   (B) How long

   (C) How well

(D) How often

18. A: What _____ is today?

    B: It's Wednesday.

    (A) weight

    (B) day

    (C) date

    (D) dead

19. A: When will the bus leave?

    B: It will leave _____ five minutes.

    (A) on (B) by (C) with (D) in

20. A: What time does the movie theater open?

    B: _____.

    (A) From Monday to Friday. (B) In 2002.

    (C) At 11 a.m. (D) By the end of this month.

答案：(A)(C)(D)(B)(C)(B)(C)(A)(A)(C)

　　　(D)(B)(C)(B)(A)(C)(D)(B)(D)(C)

Talking about Direction and Location

2 方向與位置

 本章摘要

Directions 東、南、西、北、上、下、左、右的說明

Giving Directions 市區方向及地點的說明

Extension 延伸學習

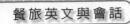
Introduction 學習重點

　　你可曾在一個陌生的城市迷路，失去了方向，不知道該往何處去呢？不管是自己出去旅遊，還是從事導遊、飯店服務人員等等工作，當客人有需要向你問路時，你能準確的說出目的地的位置，以及如何到達嗎？當你必須要介紹飯店內或是餐廳內的設施時，你能正確又簡潔的讓客人了解，並且輕易的協助他們到達要去的地方嗎？相對位置以及地點的說明，是一項重要的能力。

Useful Words 常用字彙

介係詞

介係詞	例子
in	in the restaurant
on	on the sixth floor
under	under the overpass
up	up the stairs
down	down the stairs
above	above the back door
toward	toward the gift shop
near	near the swimming pool
next to	next to the lobby

between	between the business center and the gym
in front of	in front of the restroom
behind	behind the coffee shop
on the left (side of)	on the left of the salad bar
on the right (side of)	on the right of the cash desk
at the top of	at the top of the tower
at the end of	at the end of the hall
along（沿著…）	along Park Road
opposite（在…對面）	opposite the bookstore
across from（在…對面）	across from First Avenue
A around the corner from B（從A轉個彎過去就是B）	The bookstore is around the corner from the bank
over（越過…）	over the hill

方位

	介係詞	例子
東南西北，用E、S、W、N來表示	east	the street heading east 這條街朝著東方。
	south	the car heading south 這輛車往南。
	west	the door facing west 這道門面對西方。
	north	people walking north 人們往北方走。

地點

airport	機場
boutique	精品店
bank	銀行
bookstore	書店
art museum	藝術博物館
grocery store	雜貨店
park	公園
zoo	動物園
city hall	市政府
police office	警察局
post office	郵局
shopping mall	購物中心
supermarket	超級市場
movie theater	電影院
library	圖書館
department store	百貨公司
convenient store	便利商店
hospital	醫院
clinic	診所
pharmacy	藥局
drugstore	藥妝店
bus stop	公車站

捷運／地下鐵	MRT (Mass Rapid Transit) (Taiwan) MTR(Hong Kong) the Underground (London) Subway (New York) DART(Dallas) CTA (Chicago) 以上視所在的地方，各有不同的說法。
火車站	train station
計程車招呼站	taxi stand
公路	high way
高速公路	freeway;super high way
高架橋	overpass
人行天橋	skywalk (sky bridge)
地下道	underground passage

室內設施位置及地點的說明

餐廳設施

cash desk 付款處	coffee machine 咖啡機
main dining area 主餐區	soft drink dispenser 飲料自動販賣機
salad bar 沙拉吧	women's restroom 女廁
private dining room 私人用餐區	men's restroom 男廁
smoking area 吸煙區	buffet 自助餐
non-smoking area 非吸煙區	menu 菜單

飯店設施

lobby 大廳	fitness center (gym) 健身房
elevator 電梯	swimming pool 游泳池
front desk 櫃檯	gift shop 禮品部
lounge 會客室	coffee shop 咖啡廳
banquet room 宴會廳	spa center 水療中心
business center 商務中心	massage room 按摩室
parking lot 停車場	Laundromat 自助洗衣店
casino 賭場	all-you-can-eat restaurant 吃到飽餐廳

Directions 東、南、西、北、上、下、左、右的說明

Useful Expressions 常用的表達方法

詢問地點	回答
(Excuse me,) where is_____? 不好意思，請問_____在哪裡？	Go up/down_____for _____meters. 往上 / 下走_____公尺。
How can I get to _____? 我要怎麼到_____？	Go along _____(XX Road) for _____meters. 沿著_____走_____公尺。
Can you tell me how to get to ___? 你可以告訴我怎麼到_____？	Take a left/right turn at_____. 在_____左 / 右轉。
Do you know how to get to _____? 你知道怎麼到_____？	Turn left/right when you get to ____. 當你到_____的時候，左 / 右轉。
Can you tell me where_____is? 你可以告訴我_____在哪裡嗎？	Take the elevator up/down to ____. 搭電梯往上 / 下到_____。
Do you know where _____ is ? 你知道_____在哪裡嗎？	
What' s the best way to_____? 到_____最好的路是？	
Is this the right way to_____? 這是到_____正確的路嗎？	
I' m looking for_____. 我正在尋找_____。	
I' m trying to get to_____. 我正試著要到_____。	

Conversation 會話

(*A woman is talking to a **waiter** in a restaurant.*)

Woman: Excuse me. Could you tell me where the women's restroom is, please?

Waiter: Sure. It' s on the fourth floor.

Woman: On the fourth floor?

Waiter: Yes. Go up to the fourth floor, and turn right when you get to the salad bar. You' ll see the restroom on your left. There's a sign.

Woman: Is there an elevator that I could take up to the fourth floor?

Waiter: Yes, it' s on the right side of the **smoking area**.

Woman: **Pardon me**. Can you tell me how to get to the smoking area?

Waiter: Of course. It's near the private dining room. It's on your right when you get in through the gate.

Woman: Thanks a lot. I think I can find it.

（一個女人正在跟餐廳服務生說話。）

女人：不好意思。可以請你告訴我女廁在哪裡嗎？

服務生：當然沒問題。女廁在四樓。

女人：在四樓？

服務生：是的，往上走到四樓，當你到沙拉吧的時候右轉。你會看到女廁在你的左手邊。那邊有標示。

女人：有電梯可以讓我搭到四樓嗎？

服務生：有的，電梯在吸煙區的右側。

女人：不好意思，你可以告訴我怎麼到吸煙區嗎？

服務生：當然，吸煙區就在獨立餐區的附近。就在你進大門之後的右手邊。

女人：真的太感謝你了。我想我可以找到。

Word Bank 重要單字片語

1. waiter [`wetɚ] n.（男）侍者；服務生

2. smoking area [`smokɪŋˌɛrɪə] n. phr. 吸煙區

3. Pardon me. 原諒我

Quiz 小試身手：請寫出正確英文單字

Part I

(*You are at the information desk in an American shopping center.*)

You: w_____ is the restroom, please?

Desk Clerk: It's at the end of this hallway, right n_____ t_____
（在…旁邊） the bookstore.

You: Thank you.

答案：1. Where 2. next to

Part II

(You are traveling in London and another tourist asks you for directions.)

Tourist: Excuse me. I'm i_____ f_____（尋找） the British Museum. H_____ f_____ is it from here?（離這裡多遠？）

Self: Sorry, I'm not familiar with this a_____（區域）. I myself am a t_____（旅客） here.

答案：1. looking for 2. How far 3. area 4. tourist

Giving Directions 市區方向及地點的說明

Useful Expressions 常用的表達方法

詢問地點

詢問地點	回答	
How far (away) is _____ from here? _____ 距離這邊多遠？	It's about a mile/a kilometer/three blocks (away) from _____. 距離 _____ 大約一哩／一公里／三個街區遠。	
Is there _____ around here? 這附近有_____嗎？	指引方向： 1.It's the first turn on the right/left. 這是左／右邊第一個彎。	
What's the quickest way of getting to _____? 到 _____最快的方式是？	2. Turn right/left Make a right/ left turn. 右／左轉	**at** the first/second traffic light. 在第一／第二個紅綠燈 **at** the intersection. 在十字路口 **on** _____Street/Road/Avenue. 在_____街／路／大道
What's the quickest way of getting to _____? 到 _____最快的方式是？		
Could you tell me how to get to _____? 你可以告訴我怎麼到_____嗎？	沿著某條路走： Go/Walk along _____（路名） 沿著_____走。	for	two blocks. 兩個街區 fifteen minutes. 十五分鐘 three hundred meters. 三百公尺
How do I get to _____? 我要怎麼到達 _____？		to the end of _____ Street/Road/Avenue. 到 _____街／路／大道的尾端。

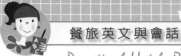

Excuse me, where is _____? 不好意思，_____在哪裡？	其他可能回答 1. Keep going. 繼續走。 2. Go that way. 走那條路。 3. You may come with me. I'm going in that direction. 你可以跟我走。我正往那個方向走。

說明地點

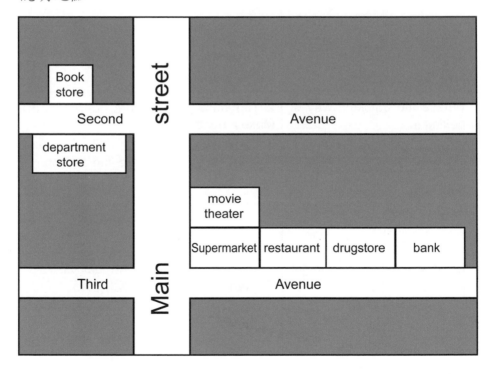

It's on_____Street/Road/ Avenue. 在_____街／路／大道。	The bookstore is on Second Avenue. 書店在第二大道上。
It's opposite/across (from) _____. 在_____對面。	The department store is across from the bookstore. 百貨公司在書店對面。
It's next to _____. 在_____旁邊。	The restaurant is next to a supermarket. 餐廳在超市隔壁。
It's on the corner of _____ and _____. 在_____及_____的轉角。	The supermarket is on the corner of Main Street and Third Avenue. 超市在大街及第三大道的轉角。
It's between_____and_____. 在_____及_____之間。	The drugstore is between a restaurant and a bank. 藥局在餐廳和銀行之間。
It's about_____minutes (by car/on foot) from here. 從這邊大約（開車／走路）_____分鐘。	It's about 30 minutes on foot from here. 從這裡步行約三十分鐘。
It's on the left/right side of _____. 在_____的左／右邊。	If you go straight along Main Street, you'll see the supermarket on the right side of a movie theater. 如果你沿著大街走，你會看到超市在電影院的右邊。

Conversation 會話

(*Jerry is talking to a hotel desk clerk and asking for directions.*)

Clerk: Jerry, How are you enjoying your time in Taipei?

Jerry: I like Taipei very much. By the way, can you **recommend** any places to visit while I'm in Taipei?

Clerk: I think Maokong would be a good **choice**. Maokong has **developed** its **unique sightseeing** and **tea tasting industry**. Students of the nearby Chengchi University **frequently hold** activities there. Lately, more and more people visit there and take the **newly** open **Maokong Gondola**.

Jerry: Sounds cool. How can I get to Maokong?

Clerk: You can take the Weshan-Neihu Line of the **Mass Rapid Transit** (**MRT**) and **get off** at Wangfang. Then take the bus No. 10 to Maokong Stop. It should take you about thirty minutes to get there.

Jerry: Thanks a lot. Also, is there a **pub** around there? I may want to go there for a drink tonight.

Clerk: Yes. Lux Pub is about a fifteen minutes walk from here. Go straight a long Heping East Road through three **traffic lights**, and when you get to Fusing South Road, go through the **intersection** and turn right. Just go south on Fusing South Road for two blocks, and you'll see the sign of Lux Pub on your left, between a **boutique** and a restaurant.

Jerry: OK. Thanks a lot.

Clerk: You're welcome.

（傑瑞正在跟飯店的櫃檯人員問路。）

櫃檯人員：傑瑞，你在台灣的這段時間愉快嗎？

傑瑞：我很喜歡台北。順便問一下，你可以推薦一下我在台北的時候可以去拜訪哪些地方嗎？

櫃檯人員：我想貓空會是一個很好的選擇。貓空已經發展了它獨特的觀光與飲茶工業。附近政治大學的學生時常在那舉辦活動。最近越來越多人拜訪那邊，並且去搭最新開幕的貓空纜車。

傑瑞：聽起來很酷。我要怎麼到貓空呢？

櫃檯人員：你可以搭捷運系統的文湖線，在萬芳站下車。然後搭十號公車到貓空站。到那邊大約花三十分鐘。

傑瑞：真的很感謝你。也問一下這附近有酒吧嗎？我今晚可能想去喝點小酒。

櫃檯人員：有的。Lux酒吧離這邊走路十五分鐘。你沿著和平東路直走，穿過三個紅綠燈，當你到復興南路的時候，穿過十字路口，然後右轉。就在復興路上往南走兩個街區，你就會看到Lux酒吧的招牌在你左邊，在一家精品店跟餐廳之間。

傑瑞：好的。很感謝你。

櫃檯人員：不客氣。

Word Bank 重要單字片語

1. recommend [ˌrɛkəˋmɛnd] v. 推薦；介紹

2. choice [tʃɔɪs] n. 選擇

3. develop [dɪˋvɛləp] v. 使成長；使發達；發展

4. unique [juˋnik] adj. 獨特的

5. sightseeing [ˋsaɪtˌsiɪŋ] n. 觀光；遊覽

6. tea tasting n. phr. 飲茶

7. industry [ˋɪndəstrɪ] n. 工業；企業；行業

8. frequently [ˋfrikwəntlɪ] adv. 頻繁地；屢次地

9. hold [hold] v. 舉行

10. newly [ˋnulɪ] adv. 新近；最近

11. Maokong Gondola 貓空纜車

12. Mass Rapid Transit (MRT) 捷運

13. get off v. phr 下車

14. pub [pʌb] n. 酒吧

15. traffic light n. phr 紅綠燈

16. intersection [ˌɪntɚˋsɛkʃən] n. 道路交叉口；十字路口

17. boutique [buˋtik] n. 精品店

Quiz 小試身手：請寫出正確英文單字

(*Some tourists stop you on the sidewalk.*)

Tourists: Excuse me, do you speak English?

Self: Sure, is there anything I can help you with?

Tourists: We're l_____ for the Moon Restaurant.

Self: M_____ a right turn at the next i_____ （十字路口） It's at the e_____ （盡頭） of the b_____ （街區） just b_____ （在…之前）the boutique. I think it's on the tenth floor, but I'm not sure.

Tourists: Thank you very much.

Self: My pleasure. Enjoy your dinner.

答案：looking, Make, intersection, end, block, before

Extension 延伸學習：台灣著名景點

National Palace Museum	故宮博物院
Taipei 101	台北101
Lungshan Temple	龍山寺
Shilin Night Market	士林夜市
Maokong Gondola	貓空纜車
Miramar Ferris Wheel	美麗華摩天輪
Taipei City Hall	台北市政府
Taipei Fine Arts Museum	台北市立美術館
Yangmingshan National Park	陽明山國家公園
Lungshan Temple	龍山寺
National Concert Hall	國家音樂廳
National Museum of History	國立歷史博物館
Sun Yat-Sen Memorial Hall	國父紀念館
Taipei Botanical Garden	植物園
Chiang Kai-Shek Memorial Hall	中正紀念堂
Leofoo Village Theme Park	六福村
Green Lake	碧潭
Sun-Moon Lake	日月潭
Fengchia Night Market	逢甲夜市
Cingjing Farm	清境農場
Lugang	鹿港
Mt. Ali (Ali Mountain)	阿里山
Anping Castle	台南安平古堡
Cheng Ching Lake	澄清湖
Love River	愛河
Chih Kan Tower	台南赤崁樓
Confucius Temple	孔廟
Hualien Ocean Park	花蓮海洋公園
Jiaosi Hot Spring	礁溪溫泉
Taroko Gorge	太魯閣
Taipinshan (Taiping Mountain)	太平山

Multiple Choice 單一選擇題

1. I live _____ Taoyuan.

   (A) on (B) at (C) in (D) under

2. There is a nice gift shop _____ Park Road.

   (A) on (B) in (C) between (D) above

3. I live three _____ away from the department store.

   (A) blocks (B) roads (C) traffic lights (D) floors

4. The restroom is on the _____of the salad bar.

   (A) along (B) front (C) left (D) west

5. I usually park my car _____ the park.

   (A) in front of (B) between (C) above (D) on

6. Mary sat _____ the tree, reading a comic book.

   (A) on   (B) under (C) above (D) across from

7. There is a river in _____ of my house.

   (A) block (B) east (C) black (D) back

8. Let's go to see "*Lust, caution*" (色戒) in the _____ on this Friday.

   (A) intersection (B) library (C) night market (D) movie theater

9. Jane is in the _____ now. The Final exam is coming next week.

   (A) bakery (B) library (C) grocery store (D) post office

10. You can go to see a doctor in a _____.

   (A) clinic (B) drugstore (C) boutique (D) lobby

11. A: Excuse me. Could you tell me where the train station is?

   B: _____

   (A) No. The train station is on Park road.

   (B) Yes. I don't know where it is.

   (C) Yes. You may come with me. I'm going in that direction.

   (D) I went to the train station last week.

12. A: Could you tell me how to get to Heping Hospital?

   B: _____

   A: Thanks anyway.

   (A) Yes. Keep going, and you'll see it on your left.

   (B) Yes. It's next to the Fusing department store.

   (C) No, it's near the MRT station.

   (D) I'm sorry. I don't know where it is.

13. A: Where is my cell phone?

   B: _____.

   A: Thank you.

   (A) It's very expensive.

   (B) It's on the table.

   (C) I bought it yesterday.

   (D) You're welcome.

14. A: _____.

   B: It's about two blocks from here.

   (A) How far is the book store from here?

   (B) How often do you go to the movie theater?

   (C) How long do you work in a hospital?

   (D) How is your work?

15. A: Where are the pineapples?

   B: _____

   (A) They sit in the non-smoking area.

   (B) They live in Taiwan.

   (C) They are in the refrigerator.

   (D) It's in the coffee machine.

請根據以下地圖，回答題組16-20題。

Book store	
Second	Avenue
department store	
movie theater	
Supermarket restaurant drugstore bank	
Third	Avenue

street

Main

16. A: Where is the restaurant?

    B: _____.

    （請選出錯誤的敘述）

    (A) It's between a supermarket and a drugstore.

    (B) It's on the Third Avenue.

    (C) It's across from a movie theater.

    (D) It's next to a supermarket.

17. (*Mary is on the Third Avenue. The restaurant is on her right side.*)

    Mary: Excuse me, how can I get to the book store?

    Stranger: _____.

    (A) Turn left on Main street. It's two blocks away from here. It will be on your right hand side.

    (B) Keep going, and you'll see it on your right.

    (C) Turn right on the Main Street, keep going for one block, and turn left. It's acroos from a department store.

    (D) Go along the Third Avenue, turn right on Main Street, and make a left turn on second Avenue. It's on the corner.

18. A: Where is the bank?

    B: _____.

    (A) It's on the corner of Main Street and Second Avenue.

    (B) It's far away from here.

(C) It's beside a drug store.

(D) It's on Second Avenue.

19. A: Where is _____?

    B: It's on the corner of Main Street and Third Avenue.

    (A) the department store (B) the movie theater (C) the bank

    (D) the supermarket

20. (*John is in front of the movie theater.*)

    John: Excuse me, I'm looking for a drug store. How can I get there?

    Stranger: _____?

    John: Yes, it right on the corner.

    Stranger: Then go to the supermarket, and turn left when you see the Third Avenue. The drugstore will be on your left.

    (A) Do you know who I am?

    (B) Do you know where the supermarket is?

    (C) Are you a tourist?

    (D) Will you take a bus there?

答案：(C)(A)(A)(C)(A)(B)(D)(D)(B)(A)
　　　(C)(D)(B)(A)(C)(C)(C)(C)(D)(B)

Hotel Service I

3 櫃檯服務（1）

 本章摘要

Receiving Guests 來訪客人的接待

Deposit 寄放與保管物品：行李寄放

Delivery 代寄郵件

Extension 延伸學習

Introduction 學習重點

　　餐旅業既屬服務業之一環，除了有形產品之外，無形產品（即服務）尤其重要。前者包括餐飲、設備（設施）、環境等，後者則是指服務而言。如何能讓前來住宿的客人，享受舒適的住宿環境及硬體設施，在與客人應對上的服務，更是能否讓客人，下一次還想再來的重要因素。如何用英語接待客人、處理寄放與保管物品、代寄郵件等服務，是本章重點。在進入本章內容之前，有一些飯店基本字彙需要知道。

Useful Words 常用字彙

旅館人員

bellboy/bellhop	行李員
doorman	門房
housekeeper	管家
maid	女服務生
manager	經理
receptionist / desk clerk	櫃台服務員
valet	侍者；泊車人員

旅館櫃檯

front desk	櫃檯
desk clerk	櫃檯接待人員
brochure	小冊子（通常為簡介或文宣）
guest	客人
elevator	電梯
room key	房間鑰匙
lobby	旅館大廳
bellboy	行李員（搬運行李的服務生）
baggage	行李
cart	推車
information Desk	服務台
reception clerk/receptionist	服務台人員
suitcase	手提箱；行李箱

住宿設備

hotel shuttle	旅館接駁車
refrigerator/fridge	冰箱
air-conditioner	冷氣
toilet paper	衛生紙（廁紙）
hair dryer	吹風機
remote (control)	遙控
lamp	燈
faucet	水龍頭
showerhead	蓮蓬頭
socket	插座

Receiving Guests 來訪客人的接待

Useful Expressions 常用的表達方法

櫃檯人員

＿＿＿＿＿＿（飯店名稱）Hotel, may I help you?	＿＿＿＿＿飯店，我能為您效勞嗎？
What dates are you looking at?	您會在哪一天到訪？

How long will you be staying?	您將會待幾天？
How many adults/children will be in the room?	有幾個大人／小孩會在房間？
Will two double beds be enough?	兩張雙人房夠嗎？
Do you want a smoking or non-smoking room?	你要吸菸房還是禁菸房？
I'm afraid we are booked on that day.	那天恐怕被訂滿了。
There are only a few vacancies left.	只剩下幾個空房了。
We advise that you book in advance during peak season.	我們建議您在旺季預先訂房。
We serve a continental breakfast. (continental breakfast 歐式早餐)	我們有提供歐式早餐。
Cable television is included, but the movie channel is extra.	有線電視有包含其中，但電影頻道是另外的。

客人

Is this _____ Hotel?	這是_____飯店嗎？
I'd like to make a reservation for next week.	我想要訂下週的房間。
Is it necessary to book ahead?	有必要事先訂房嗎？
Do you have any vacancies?	你們有任何空房嗎？
Do you do group bookings?	你們有在辦理團體訂房嗎？
When is it considered off- season?	什麼時候被視為淡季？
Do you charge extra for two beds?	多加兩張床需要額外付費嗎？
Do you have any cheaper rooms?	有任何更便宜的房間嗎？
What's the rate for_____ 房型 (e.g. a single room)? 註:房型的介紹請見第八章。	_____房的價錢是多少？
Do you offer free breakfast? /Does my stay here include breakfast?	你們有提供免費早餐嗎？ / 在這住房含早餐嗎？
Is there _____設施 (e.g. a restaurant, an outdoor pool...) in the hotel?	在飯店裡有_____（設施）嗎？
Do you allow pets?	你們允許攜帶寵物嗎？
Is smoking allowed in the hotel?	飯店裡允許抽煙嗎？
Do the rooms have_____房間設備(e.g. refrigerators, televisions...)?	房間有_____（設備）嗎？
Do you have _____房間設備 (e.g. air conditioning...) in the rooms?	在房間裡有_____（房間設備）嗎？

Conversation 1 會話一

(A guest is asking for a room.)

Receptionist: Good afternoon. May I help you?

Guest: Yes, please. Do you have any rooms **available**?

Receptionist: Yes. Would you like a double or a single room?

Guest: A double room, please. Are the beds **full sized**?

Receptionist: Yes, they are. Our single rooms have **king sized** beds.

Guest: How much would it be for three nights?

Receptionist: It's NT$ 4800 per night. It would cost you NT$ 14400 for all three days.

Guest: I would like to pay by credit card.

Receptionist: Of course. We take Visa and American Express. Could you **fill out** this form, please?

Guest: Do I need to write down my **passport number**?

Receptionist: No, just your **signature** and address.

(The guest fills in the form.)

Guest: Here you are.

Receptionist: Here's your key. Your room number is 518.

Guest: Thank you.

Receptionist: Thank you very much. If you need anything, please **dial** 9 for the **receptionist**. Enjoy your stay!

（一個客人正在詢問住房事宜。）

櫃檯人員：午安，我能為您服務嗎？

客人：是的。你們有空房嗎？

櫃檯人員：是的，有。請問您要雙人房還是單人房？

客人：雙人房，謝謝。床是加大型的嗎？

櫃檯人員：是的。我們的單人房有加大型的床。

客人：三個晚上要多少錢？

櫃檯人員：一個晚上四千八百元。三天總共一萬四千四百元。

客人：我想用信用卡付帳。

櫃檯人員：當然。我們接受威士卡以及美國運通卡。可以請您填這個表格嗎？

客人：我需要寫我的護照號碼嗎？

櫃檯人員：不用，只要簽名跟地址。

（客人填寫表格。）

客人：給你。

櫃檯人員：這是您的鑰匙。您的房號是518。

客人：謝謝。

櫃檯人員：非常感謝您。

客人：如果您需要任何東西，請打分機9找櫃檯人員。住房愉快！

Word Bank 重要單字片語

1. available [ə`veləbḷ] adj. 可用的；有空的

2. full sized 大型的

3. king sized 超過標準長度的；加大的

4. fill out... (the form) v. phr. 填寫…（表格）

5. passport number [`pæs͵port`nʌmbɚ] n. phr. 護照號碼

6. signature [`sɪgnətʃɚ] n. 簽名

7. address [`ædrɛs] n. 住址；地址

8. dial [`daɪəl] v. 撥號；打電話

9. receptionist [rɪ`sɛpʃənɪst] n. 櫃台接待員

Conversation 2 會話二

(*A **potential** guest is asking about room types on the phone.*)

Receptionist: Good morning, Tiger Hotel. How may I help you?

Guest: Good morning. What types of rooms do you **offer**?

Receptionist: We have all types of **accommodations** available. How many people will be traveling with you?

Guest: There are four in my **party**, two **adults** and two **children**.

Receptionist: There are regular, deluxe, and superior room you can choose from.

Guest: Do you have any rooms with nice **views**?

Receptionist: We have rooms with ocean or **harbor** side rooms.

Guest: Is there an **extra charge** for a child's bed?

Receptionist: Not for superior rooms. There is NT 300 per night charge for regular rooms or NT\$ 500 charge for deluxe rooms.

（一個可能的客人正透過電話詢問房間類型。）

櫃檯人員：早安，這裡是泰格飯店。我可以怎麼幫忙您呢？

客人：早安。你們提供什麼樣的房間？

櫃檯人員：我們有各種客房。有多少人會跟您同行？

客人：我們這群有四個人，兩個大人，兩個小孩。

櫃檯人員：有普通、豪華以及精緻客房供您選擇。

客人：你們有視野好的房間嗎？

櫃檯人員：我們有海景或港邊房間。

客人：小孩的床有額外收費嗎？

櫃檯人員：精緻客房沒有。普通客房一晚多收三百元，豪華客房多收五百元。

Word Bank 重要單字片語

1. potential [pə`tɛnʃəl] adj. 潛在的；可能的

2. offer [`ɔfɚ] v. 給予；提供

3. accommodation [ə͵kamə`deʃən] n. 住處；膳宿

4. party [`partɪ] n. 一夥人；一行人

5. adult [ə`dʌlt] n. 成年人

6. children [`tʃɪldrən] n. 小孩（單數為child）

7. view [vju] n. 景觀

8. harbor [`harbɚ] n. 港灣；海港

9. extra [`ɛkstrə] adj. 額外的；另外收費的

10. charge [tʃardʒ] n. 費用

Conversation 3 會話三

(Mary is making a reservation for a hotel room over the phone.)

Receptionist: Milton Hotel. Can I help you?

Mary: Yes, I'd like to make a reservation for tomorrow. Do you have any rooms available?

Receptionist: We have three rooms available. I'm seeing two doubles and one single. Which kind of room would you like?

Mary: A single room, please.

Receptionist: How long will you stay, ma'am?

Mary: Two days. Could you tell me what **amenities** would be available with the room?

Receptionist: Room amenities include a TV with **cable** where we do offer the newest **selection** of movies via **Pay-Per-View** as well as our own hotel **broadcast**. Internet

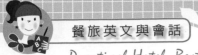

can also be **provided** upon **request**. **Additionally**, **room service** is available 24 hours a day. We also provide a refrigerator with drinks. Our hotel amenities include a pool, fitness center, and a restaurant on the first floor.

Mary: Do you provide **toiletries** such as **shampoo** and **toothpaste**?

Receptionist: Yes, **along with toothbrushes**, **soap**, **shower caps** and **lotion**.

Mary: Is there **beer** in the fridge?

Receptionist: Room service can send some up if you would like to order this.

Mary: What's the price of the single room?

Receptionist: Your room will be a total of NT$ 3200 dollars plus tax.

Mary: Are any **meals included**?

Receptionist: Yes, we have a **complementary breakfast buffet** in our restaurant.

Mary: That's good.

Receptionist: May I have your name, please?

Mary: Yes. Mary Smith.

Receptionist: Thank you Ms. Smith. You've made a reservation for a single room for two days. We'll be **looking forward to** your **arrival**.

Mary: Thanks for your **patience**.

（瑪莉正打電話訂房。）

櫃檯人員：米爾頓飯店。我能為您效勞嗎？

瑪莉：是的，我想訂明天的房間。你們有空房嗎？

櫃檯人員：我們還有三間空房。現在看到兩間雙人房和一間單人房。您想要什麼樣的房間？

瑪莉：單人房，謝謝。

櫃檯人員：您會待多久呢，女士？

瑪莉：兩天。你可以告訴我房間裡有什麼設備嗎？

櫃檯人員：房間設施包括有線電視，我們提供最新的付費電影，也有我們飯店所播放的。網路經過要求也可提供。另外，客房服務是二十四小時提供。我們也提供冰箱，裡面附有飲料。我們飯店設施包括游泳池、健身中心、以及餐廳在一樓。

瑪莉：你們有提供盥洗用具像是洗髮精和牙膏？

櫃檯人員：有的，另外還有牙刷、肥皂、浴帽和乳液。

瑪莉：冰箱裡有啤酒嗎？

櫃檯人員：如果你需要的話，客房服務部可以派人送上去。

瑪莉：單人房的價錢怎麼算？

櫃檯人員：您的房間含稅將是三千兩百元。

瑪莉：有包括任何餐點嗎？

櫃檯人員：是的我們在餐廳有自助式的免費早餐。

瑪莉：那很好。

櫃檯人員：請問可以告訴我您的姓名嗎？

瑪莉：可以。瑪莉‧史密斯。

櫃檯人員：謝謝您，史密斯女士。您訂了兩天單人房。我將期待您的
到來。

瑪莉：感謝您的耐心。

Word Bank 重要單字片語

1. amenity [ə`mɛnətɪ] n. 便利設施（常用複數形式）

2. cable [`kebḷ] n. 有線電視

3. selection [sə`lɛkʃən] n. 選擇

4. Pay-Per-View 收費的電視節目

5. broadcast [`brɔdˌkæst] n. 播放

6. provide [prə`vaɪd] v. 提供

7. request [rɪ`kwɛst] n. v. 要求；請求

8. additionally [ə`dɪʃənḷɪ] adv. 附加地；同時；此外

9. room service n. phr. 客房服務

10. toiletries [`tɔɪlətrɪs] n. 盥洗用品

11. shampoo [ʃæm`pu] n. 洗髮精

12. toothpaste [`tuθˌpest] n. 牙膏

13. along with 與…在一起；在…以外

14. toothbrush [ˋtuθˏbrʌʃ] n. 牙刷

15. soap [sop] n. 肥皂

16. shower cap [ˋʃaʊɚˏkæp] n. phr. 浴帽

17. lotion [ˋloʃən] n. 乳液

18. beer [bɪr] n. 啤酒

19. meal [mil] n. 餐點

20. include [ɪnˋklud] v. 包括；包含

21. complementary breakfast [ˏkampləˋmɛntərɪˋbrɛkfəst] n. 免費早餐

22. buffet [bəˋfe] n. 自助餐

23. look forward to v. phr. 期待

24. arrival [əˋraɪvl̩] n. 到達

25. patience [ˋpeʃəns] n. 耐心

Quiz 小試身手：請寫出正確英文單字

1. Q: Do you have any rooms a_____?

   A: Yes, we have all types of a_____ which you can choose from.

2. Guest: I would like to r_____ a room with an ocean v_____.

   Clerk: Okay, how many people are you t_____ with?

3. Clerk: How l_____ would you stay? Guest: Three days.

答案：available, accommodations, reserve, view, traveling, long

Deposit 寄放與保管物品：行李寄放

Useful Expressions 常用的表達方法

貴重物品

電子設備	laptop/notebook	手提電腦
	MP3 player	MP3播放器
	cell phone	手機
	digital camera	數位相機
文件	passport	護照
	plane ticket	機票
	visa	簽證
	contract	合約
金錢	cash	現金
	traveler's check	旅行支票
	credit card	信用卡
珠寶	ring	戒指
	earrings	耳環
	bracelet	手環
	necklace	項鍊
其他	bag/baggage	包包 / 行李
	briefcase	公事包
	key	鑰匙
	purse/wallet	皮包 / 皮夾

Conversation 1 會話一

(*John wants to **deposit** his **valuables** in the hotel. Now, he is talking to a hotel desk clerk.*)

Desk Clerk: Can I help you?

John: Yes. Could I deposit my **diamond earrings** in the hotel's **safekeeping**?

Desk Clerk: Certainly, sir. I can help you put it in our **safe-deposit** box. Additionally, we have free use of **safe**-deposit box in all our rooms for **convenience's sake**.

John: Oh, I didn't know that. I think I'll try that first. Thanks for telling me.

Desk Clerk: No problem.

（約翰想把他的貴重物品寄放在飯店。他現在正在跟一位飯店櫃檯人員說話。）

櫃檯人員：我可以為您效勞嗎？

約翰：是的。我可以把我的鑽石耳環寄放在飯店的保管處嗎？

櫃檯人員：當然，先生。我可以幫您放在保險箱裡。另外，為了方便起見，我們所有的房間都有免費的保險箱可使用。

約翰：喔，我之前不知道。我想我會先試試房間裡的保險箱。謝謝你告訴我。

櫃檯人員：不客氣。

Word Bank 重要單字片語

1. deposit [dɪ`pazɪt] v. 放置；寄存

2. valuables [`væljuəblz] n. 貴重物品；財產

3. diamond [`daɪəmənd] n. 鑽石

4. earrings [`ɪrˏrɪŋz] n. 耳環

5. safekeeping [`sefˏkɪpɪŋ] n. 保管處

6. safe-deposit box n. 防火保險箱

7. safe [sef] n. 保險箱

8. convenience [kən`vinjəns] n. 方便；合宜

9. sake [sek] n. 目的；理由

Conversation 2 會話二

(*Lisa wants to **store** her bags for a few days. She is talking to a **bellhop**.*)

Lisa: Hello. I want to store my two bags for four days.

Bellhop: Okay. We **require** a credit card number for a **deposit**. You need to pay NT 100 dollars per day plus tax.

Lisa: Okay. When do I pay? Now?

Bellhop: You can pay when you **pick up** your bags. You also need to sign this form, please.

(*Lisa signs the form.*)

Bellhop: I'll need to check your ID, please.

(*The bellhop checks the ID.*)

Bellhop: Okay. Please keep the number **tag**.

Lisa: Thank you.

（麗莎想要把他的包包寄放個幾天。她正在跟一位行李員說話。）
麗莎：哈囉。我想要把我的包包寄放個四天。
行李員：好的。我們需要信用卡號碼做為訂金。您一天需要付一百元
　　　　含稅。
麗莎：好的。我什麼時候需要付清？現在嗎？

行李員：您可以在拿回您的包包時付清。您還需要在這個表格簽名。

（麗莎在表格上簽名。）

行李員：我需要看一下您的身分證明。

（行李員檢查身分證明。）

行李員：好的。請保存好這個數字吊牌。

麗莎：謝謝。

Word Bank 重要單字片語

1. store [stɔr] v. 保管；收存
2. bellhop [`bɛl‚hap] n. 行李員
3. require [rɪ`kwaɪr] v. 需要；要求
4. deposit [dɪ`pazɪt] n. 保證金；押金；訂金
5. pick up v. phr. 拾起；收拾
6. tag [tæg] n. 牌子；標籤

Conversation 3 會話三

(*Lisa wants to take back her stored **luggage**. She is talking to a desk clerk.*)

Lisa: I would like to pick up my stored luggage.

Desk Clerk: Let me see your number tag and your ID, please.

Lisa: Here they are. What's the **total cost**?

Desk Clerk: It **comes to** NT 400 with tax.

（麗莎想要拿回寄放的包包。她正在跟櫃檯人員說話。）

麗莎：我想要取回我所寄放的包包。

櫃檯人員：請讓我看看您的數字吊牌以及身分證明。

麗莎：給你。總共的費用是多少？

櫃檯人員：共計四百元含稅。

Word Bank 重要單字片語

1. luggage [ˋlʌgɪdʒ] n. [U] 行李

2. total [ˋtotl̩] adj. 總計的；總括的

3. cost [kɔst] n. 費用

4. come to v. phr. 共計…

Quiz 小試身手：請寫出正確英文單字

1. If you want to store your v_____ （珍貴物品）, such as diamond n_____ （項鍊） or l_____ （手提電腦）, you can d_____ （存放） them in a hotel.

2. If you want to store your bags, you may need c_____ cards （信用卡） and remember to keep the l_____ t_____（行李吊牌）.

答案：valuables, necklace, laptop, deposit, credits, luggage, tag

Delivery Service 代寄郵件

Useful Expressions 常用的表達方法

郵件的相關用詞

stamp	郵票
airmail	空運
registered/certified mail ordinary mail express mail package/parcel postcard	掛號郵件 平信 快遞郵件 包裹 明信片
bulk rate book rate	大宗郵件費率 印刷品費率
zip code	郵遞區號
postage/postal charge postmark postal	郵資 郵戳 郵政的
post officer/mail man mailbox	郵差 郵筒
fragile	易碎的

詢問 / 寄郵件

英文	中文
How much is the postage?	郵資多少錢？
When will it arrive?	何時會到達？
Does the hotel provide delivery services?	飯店有提供遞送服務嗎？
What is the quickest/cheapest kind of mail?	哪一種方式是最快 / 最便宜的？
I need this sent overseas.	我需要把這個寄到國外。

Conversation 1 會話一

(*A guest wants to send a letter. He is talking to a clerk.*)

Desk Clerk: Good morning, sir. How can I help you?

Guest: Yes. I want to send this letter by **ordinary** mail and this **postcard** by **airmail**.

Desk Clerk: Okay. The **postage** will be added to your bill. Is that alright?

Guest: Sure. No problem.

（一位客人想要寄信。他正在和櫃檯人員說話。）

櫃檯人員：早安，先生。我可以為您效勞嗎？

客人：是的。我想要這封信用平信、這張明信片用航空信寄出。

櫃檯人員：好的。郵資將會加到您的帳單，可以嗎？

客人：當然。沒問題。

Word Bank 重要單字片語

1. ordinary [ˋɔrdṇ͵ɛrɪ] adj. 普通的
2. postcard [ˋpost͵kard] n. 明信片
3. airmail [ˋɛr͵mel] n. 航空郵件
4. postage [ˋpostɪdʒ] n. [U] 郵資；郵費

Conversation 2 會話二

(*A guest wants to send a package overseas. He is talking to a desk clerk.*)

Guest: I need this package sent **overseas**.

Desk Clerk: Where to?

Guest: To the U.K.

(*The clerk **weighs** the package.*)

Desk Clerk: The **postal** charge will be $ 7.45. (US. dollars)

Guest: Is that Global Air Mail?

Desk Clerk: Yes.

Guest: When will it arrive?

Desk Clerk: Four to ten days.

Guest: Thank you.

（客人想要寄一個包裹到國外。他正在跟櫃檯人員說話。）

客人：我需要把這個包裹寄到國外。

櫃檯人員：寄到哪裡？

客人：到英國。

（櫃檯人員在秤包裹的重量。）

櫃檯人員：郵資一共是7.45元。（美元）

客人：這是全球航空郵件嗎？

櫃檯人員：是的。

客人：什麼時候會到達？

櫃檯人員：四到十天。

客人：謝謝。

Word Bank 重要單字片語

1. overseas [ˋovɚˋsɪz] adv. 海外；國外

2. weigh [we] v. 稱…的重量

3. postal [ˋpostl̩] adj. 郵政的；郵件的

Quiz 小試身手：請寫出正確英文單字

Guest: I want to send a p_____ o_____（我想寄包裹到國外）by

a_____.

Clerk: Sure, I'll w_____ it first. Please wait for a second. The

p_____ c_____ will be 500 NT dollars.

答案：package, overseas, airmail, weigh, postal, charge

 Extension 延伸學習：旅館類型

(youth) hostel	青年旅舍
bed-and-breakfast(B&B)	家庭式旅館
cabin	小屋
guesthouse	家庭旅館（民宿）
inn	小旅館；小飯店
lodge	休閒遊樂區的旅館
motel	汽車旅館
cottage	鄉間小屋
resort	度假屋
villa	別墅

Multiple Choice 單一選擇題

1. It's a _____ room, and the bed is a little small.

   (A) cart (B) name (C) single (D) big

2. If you send it by _____, it will be very expensive.

   (A) e-mail (B) airmail (C) earrings (D) deposit

3. You will enjoy staying in greatest _____ in Las Vegas.

   (A) room (B) bags   (C) carts (D) accommodations

4. My husband is very tall. Do you have _____ beds?

   (A) kid sized (B) king sized (C) small sized (D) middle sized

5. You need to pay the _____ according to the weight of your package.

   (A) postage (B) age (C) postal (D) letter

6. How much does this package _____?

   (A) deposit (B) tag (C) fill (D) weigh

7. A _____is the person who welcomes and helps guests in a hotel.

   (A) bellhop   (B) manager (C) receptionist (D) housekeeper

8. Please _____ out the register form, sir.

   (A) apologize (B) order (C) fill (D) make

9. We have single_____ available at the moment.

   (A) room (B) our rooms (C) the room (D) rooms

10. I'd _____ reserve a room in your hotel.

(A) like to (B) want to (C) ask for (D) need of

11. I've made a _____ for a room at that hotel on July 3rd.

(A) receptionist (B) check (C) reservation (D) dish

12. We look forward _____ seeing your family.

(A) with (B) to (C) for (D) on

13. Jimmy: _____

Receptionist: NT$2,200.

(A) How would you like your job?

(B) Do you have any room available on April 16th?

(C) What's the date today?

(D)How much is a double room for one night?

14. Receptionist: Good evening, sir. _____

Jim: No, we don't.

(A) Do you have a reservation, sir?

(B) Where do you come from, sir?

(C) Do you accept personal check?

(D) What kind of room do you want?

15. Receptionist: Yes. What kind of room do you want?

Guest:_____, please.

(A) A cup of tea

(B) A beef hamburger

(C) A double room

(D) Non-smoking

16. A: Good morning, East Hotel. _____

B: I'd like to reserve a single room.

(A) How would you like to pay?

(B) When will you arrive at out hotel?

(C) Where are you from?

(D) May I help you?

17. Joanna: I'd like to check in, please.

Receptionist: _____

Joanna: Joanna Lin.

(A) Would you please fill out the form?

(B) Do you want to order something to drink?

(C) May I have your name, please?

(D) Would you like a single room?

18. Guest: _____

Desk Clerk: Four to ten days.

Guest: Thank you.

(A) How much is the postage?

(B) When will it arrive?

(C) When do I pay?

(D) Could I deposit my diamond necklace in the hotel's

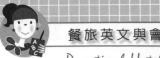
safekeeping?

19. Desk Clerk: How can I help you, ma'am?

Lisa: _____

Desk Clerk: Let me see your number tag and your ID, please.

(A) I've got to go.

(B) I'd like to pay by credit card.

(C) I need a towel.

(D) I would like to pick up my stored luggage.

20. Receptionist: Here's your key. Your room number is 319. If you need anything, please dial 9 for the receptionist.

_____

Guest: Thank you.

(A) Enjoy your stay!

(B) Enjoy your meal!

(C) It's my pleasure.

(D) I'll be right back.

答案：(C)(B)(D)(B)(A)(D)(C)(C)(D)(A)

(C)(B)(D)(A)(C)(D)(C)(B)(D)(A)

Hotel Service II

4 櫃檯服務（2）

本章摘要

Checking into a Hotel and a Wake Up Call 住宿手續的登記和晨喚服務

Laundry Service 洗衣服務

Parking and Taxi Dispatch 停車與叫車服務

Lost and Found 失物招領

Extension 延伸學習

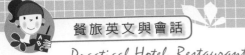

餐旅英文與會話

Practical Hotel, Restaurant, and Travel English

Introduction 學習重點

　　延續上一章，本章有關櫃檯服務的重點有住宿手續的登記（check in）、晨喚服務（wake up call）、洗衣服務（laundry service）、停車與叫車服務（calling for a taxi）、失物招領（lost and found）。

Useful Words 常用字彙

旅館房間種類

deluxe room	豪華客房
diplomatic suite	外交官套房
double room	雙人房
executive suite	行政主管套房
ocean view suite	海景套房
presidential suite/penthouse	總統套房
single room	單人房
suite	套房（臥室、客廳、浴室成套的房間）
twin (bed) room	雙人房（兩張單人床）
superior room	超級房
regular room	一般房
standard room	標準房
adjoining room	兩房中間有門連接的房間

住宿設備

hotel shuttle	旅館接駁車
refrigerator/fridge	冰箱
air-conditioner	冷氣
toilet paper	衛生紙（廁紙）
hair dryer	吹風機
remote (control)	遙控
lamp	燈
faucet	水龍頭

床的類型

single bed	單人床
double bed	一張雙人床
queen sized bed	標準床
king sized bed	加大床
twin beds	兩張單人床；對床
bunk beds	上下舖
camp bed	輕便帆步床
extra bed	加床
rollaway bed (cot)	床底下加輪子可移動或摺疊者
sofa bed, pull-out couch	沙發床

Checking into a Hotel and a Wake Up Call

住宿手續的登記和晨喚服務

Useful Expressions 常用的表達方法

櫃檯人員

What name is the reservation under?	是用誰的名字預約的？
Are you planning on checking out tomorrow?	你計畫明天要辦理退房嗎？
I'm afraid you can't check in until after 4:00 pm.	恐怕你要到四點之後才能辦理登記入宿。
Complimentary breakfast is served in the from to 8 to 10 am. (complimentary breakfast 免費招待的早餐)	免費早餐將會八點到十點在大廳提供。
Just call the front desk if you need any extra pillows or towels.	如果你另外需要枕頭跟毛巾，只要打電話給櫃檯人員即可。
The dining room is open from 5 pm until 9 pm.	飯廳從下午五點開到九點。

客人

We have a reservation under Dana Young.	我們有用唐娜‧楊的名字訂房。
What time is the pool open until? What time does your swimming pool open?	游泳池開到幾點？ 你們的游泳池幾點開？

What time is breakfast served? When is breakfast served?	早餐什麼時候開始供餐？
Is it too early to check in?	現在辦理登記入宿是不是太早了？
When is our check-out time?	你們辦理退宿的時間是？
Can we get a wake-up call?	我們能不能有叫醒起床的服務？
Do you have a shuttle bus to the airport?	你們有交通接駁車到機場嗎？
Where is the shuttle bus?	那裡有交通接駁車？
How long is the ride?	路程多久？
Does your hotel have wireless internet service?	你們飯店有無線網路的服務嗎？

Conversation 1 會話一

(*Dana is checking into a hotel.*)

Dana: Hi. I'd like to check in.

Desk Clerk: Good evening, Ma'am. Do you have a reservation with us?

Dana: Yes. My name is Dana Young.

Desk Clerk: Ms. Young. You reserved a double room with a **mountain** view.

Dana: Yes. I'm with my husband. I'd like to have a room on the top floor.

Desk Clerk: Let me check. Room 928. Please fill out this **registration** card, including your name, address, number of people, credit card type and number, signature, and **expiration date**.

(*Dana fills in the form.*)

Desk Clerk: How would you like to make the **payment**?

Dana: Do you take American Express?

Desk Clerk: We do.

(*Dana hands the card over.*)

Desk Clerk: Thank you, ma'am. Here are your key and **breakfast voucher**. If you pass that door and turn left, you'll see an elevator. Your room will be on your right hand side when you walk out of the elevator.

Dana: Thank you.

（唐娜正在辦理登記入宿。）

唐娜：嗨。我想要辦理登記入宿。

櫃檯人員：晚安，小姐。您有先跟我們預約嗎？

唐娜：有的，我的名字是唐娜‧楊。

櫃檯人員：楊小姐，您預訂了山景的雙人房。

唐娜：是的，我跟我丈夫一起。我想要一間頂樓的房間。

櫃檯人員：讓我看看。928房。 請您填寫這張入宿登記卡，包括名字、地址、人數、信用卡類型與號碼、簽名以及到期日期。

（唐娜填寫表格。）

櫃檯人員：請問您要用什麼付款方式？

唐娜：你們接受美國運通卡嗎？

櫃檯人員：我們接受。

（唐娜把卡遞給櫃檯人員。）

櫃檯人員：謝謝您，小姐。這是您的鑰匙及早餐券。如果您經過那扇門接著左轉，您將會看到電梯。當您走出電梯之後，您的房間將會在您的右手邊。

唐娜：謝謝。

Word Bank 重要單字片語

1. mountain [ˋmauntn̩] n. 山

2. registration [ˌrɛdʒɪˋstreʃən] n. 登記；註冊

3. expiration date [ˌɛkspəˋreʃən det] n. phr. 到期日；截止期

4. payment [ˋpemənt] n. 支付；付款

5. breakfast voucher [ˋbrɛkfəstˋvautʃɚ] n. phr. 早餐券

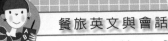

Conversation 2 會話二

(*Dana is calling room service for a wake up call.*)

Dana: Hello. This is room 928.

Clerk: Hello, room service. How can I help you, ma'am?

Dana: Could you do me a **favor**? I need a wake up call at 6:30 tomorrow morning.

Clerk: I certainly can.

Dana: When will breakfast be offered?

Clerk: You can have breakfast from 6 to 10 a.m.

Dana: Thank you.

（唐娜正在打電話給客房服務要求喚醒起床的服務。）

唐娜：哈囉。這是928房。

櫃檯人員：哈囉，客房服務。我能為您做什麼，女士？

唐娜：你可以幫我一個忙嗎？我需要明天早上六點半叫我起床。

櫃檯人員：當然可以。

唐娜：早餐幾點供應？

櫃檯人員：您可以在早上六點到十點用早餐。

唐娜：謝謝你。

Word Bank 重要單字片語

1. favor [ˋfevɚ] n. 恩惠

Quiz 小試身手：請寫出正確英文單字

Guest: Good Morning. I'd like to c_____ i____（辦理入住手續）.

Desk Clerk: Good evening, Ma'am. Do you have a r_____（預約）with us?

Dana: Yes. My name is Luis Wang.

Desk Clerk: Ms. Wang. You reserved a s_____ room（單人房）with a m_____ view（山景）.

Dana: Yes.

Desk Clerk: Let me check. Room 928. Please f_____ out（填寫）this r_____（住宿；登記）card, including your name, address, number of people, credit card type and number, s_____（簽名）, and e_____ date（到期日）.

答案：check, in, reservation, single, mountain, fill, registration, signature, expiration

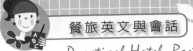
Laundry Service 洗衣服務

Useful Expressions 常用的表達方法

衣服種類

blouse	女用襯衫；短上衣
dress	洋裝
skirt	裙
sweater	毛衣
t-shirt	圓領衫
shirt	襯衫
coat	外套
suit	套裝
jeans	牛仔衣褲
trousers	較正式的西褲
pants	褲子
shorts	短褲
slacks	寬鬆的長褲
vest	背心
tank top	運動背心

Conversation 會話

*(Dana is calling to housekeeping to ask about laundry service hours and **reception procedures**.)*

Dana: Good afternoon. I'd like to know about your laundry services.

Clerk: If your **laundry** is received before 9 a.m., we will **deliver** it to your room by 4 p.m. the same day. If you are **in a hurry**, we have a three hour quick service.

Dana: What are your rates?

Clerk: That rate **chart** is on the table of your **dressing table**, ma'am.

Dana: Oh, I see. Thank you. Could you send someone to room 928 to pick up some laundry for me, please?

Clerk: Sure. I'll send someone **immediately**. He will be there in a few minutes.

(*After a few minutes...*)

Housekeeper: Housekeeping. May I come in?

Dana: Yes, I want to have this laundry done.

Housekeeper: Certainly, ma'am. Would you please fill out the laundry form first?

Dana: Where is it?

Housekeeper: It's in the **drawer** of your dressing table.

Dana: Sure. May I use your pen?

Housekeeper: Certainly, ma'am. Here you are.

Dana: By the way, I'd like this **sweater** washed by hand in cold water. It might **shrink otherwise**. Besides, the two **shirts** are not for washing but for **pressing** only.

Housekeeper: Sweaters by hand in cold water and shirts for pressing only. I see. We'll deliver them tomorrow noon around 12.

Dana: Great. Thank you.

（唐娜正打電話到客房管理部去詢問有關於洗衣服務的時間以及受理程序的問題。）

唐娜：午安。我想要了解有關洗衣服務的事情。

櫃檯人員：如果您送洗的衣服在上午九點前送洗，我們會在當天下午四點前送到您的房間。如果您很急的話，我們有三小時的快速服務。

唐娜：你們費用怎麼算？

櫃檯人員：小姐，費用表在您的梳妝台上。

唐娜：喔，我懂了。可以請你派一個人到928房來幫我拿要送洗的衣服嗎？

櫃檯人員：當然好。我會馬上派人上去。他會在幾分鐘之後就到。

（在幾分鐘之後…）

房務員：客房服務。請問我可以進去嗎？

唐娜：可以，我想要送洗這些衣服。

房務員：好的，小姐。可以請您先填寫洗衣表格嗎？

唐娜： 在哪裡？

房務員：表格在您梳妝台的抽屜。

唐娜：好，我可以用你的筆嗎？

房務員：當然，小姐。給您。

唐娜：對了，這件毛衣用冷水手洗。不然他可能會縮水。另外，那兩件襯衫不用洗，只要燙就好。

房務員：毛衣用冷水手洗，襯衫只要燙。我懂了，我會在大約明天中午十二點左右送回來。

唐娜：太好了。謝謝你。

Word Bank 重要單字片語

1. reception [rɪ`sɛpʃən] n. 接待；接受

2. procedure [prə`sidʒɚ] n. 程序；手續；步驟

3. laundry [`lɔndrɪ] n. 送洗的衣服

4. deliver [dɪ`lɪvɚ] v. 投遞；傳送；運送

5. in a hurry 匆匆

6. chart [tʃart] n. 圖表

7. dressing table [`drɛsɪŋ`tebl̩] n. phr. 梳妝臺；鏡臺

8. immediately [ɪ`midɪɪtlɪ] adv. 立即；即刻

9. drawer [`drɔɚ] n. 抽屜

10. sweater [`swɛtɚ] n. 毛線衣

11. shrink [ʃrɪŋk] v. 收縮；縮短；皺縮

12. otherwise [`ʌðɚˌwaɪz] adv. 否則；不然

13. shirt [ʃɝt] n. 襯衫

14. press [prɛs] v. 熨平（衣服）

Quiz 小試身手：請寫出正確英文單字

Guest: I'd like this d_____（洋裝）washed b_____ h_____
（手洗）in cold water, or it might s_____. Besides, the two
b_____（女用襯衫）are not for w_____（洗）but for
p_____（燙）only.

Housekeeper: I see. We'll d_____（遞送）them tomorrow noon.

答案：dress, by, hand, shrink, blouses, washing, pressing, deliver

Parking and Taxi Dispatch 停車與叫車服務

Useful Expressions 常用的表達方法

泊車人員

1. I'll call a taxi dispatch for you.

   我幫您打電話給計程車行派車來。

2. They will pull up to the front there so you may take a seat until they arrive.

   他們會把車停在前面那裡，所以在他們來之前，您可以坐一下。

Conversation 1 會話一

(*A **valet** is going to **park** for Dana.*)

Valet: Good morning, ma'am. May I help you?

Dana: Yes. Here is the key, thanks.

Valet: This is your **claim** ticket. Please bring it with you when you leave.

Dana: I got it. Thanks a lot.

（一名泊車人員正要幫唐娜停車。）

泊車人員：早安，小姐。我可以為您效勞嗎？

唐娜：是的。這是車鑰匙。謝謝。

泊車人員：這是您的領車券。當您要離開的時候請帶著這張券。

唐娜：我明白了，非常感謝。

Word Bank 重要單字片語

1. valet [`vælɪt] n. 泊車人員
2. park [pɑrk] v. 停放（車）
3. claim [klem] n. 所有權；索回

Conversation 2 會話二

(*Dana wants to call for a* **taxi**. *She is talking to a desk clerk.*)

Dana: Good morning. I need a **cab** to take me to the airport.

Desk Clerk: I'll call a taxi **dispatch** for you. May I have your name, please?

Dana: Dana Young.

Desk Clerk: (*The clerk is talking on the phone.*)—Hi, this is Milton Hotel. We need a cab to the airport.

Desk Clerk: (*The clerk is talking to Dana.*) They will **pull up** to the

front there so you may **take a seat** until they arrive.
Your cab will arrive in ten minutes.

Dana: Thanks a lot.

（唐娜想要打電話叫計程車。她正在跟一個櫃檯人員講話。）

唐娜：早安。我需要一台計程車載到我機場。

櫃檯人員：我幫您打電話給計程車行。可以請問您的名字嗎？

唐娜：唐娜‧楊。

櫃檯人員：（櫃檯人員正在講電話）喂，這邊是米爾頓飯店。我們需
要一台計程車到機場。

櫃檯人員：（櫃檯人員正在跟唐娜說話）他們會把車停在前面那裡，
所以在他們來之前，您可以坐一下。您的計程車將在十分
鐘後到達。

唐娜：謝謝你。

Word Bank 重要單字片語

1. taxi [ˋtæksɪ] n. 計程車

2. cab [kæb] n. 計程車

3. dispatch [dɪˋspætʃ] n. 派遣；發送

4. pull up v. phr. 停下來

5. take a seat v. phr. 坐一下

Quiz 小試身手：請寫出正確英文單字

Valet: Good morning, sir. M_____ I help you?

Guest: Yes. Here is the k_____.

Valet: This is your c_____ t_____ (領車券). Please bring it with
you when you're leaving.

答案：May, key, claim, ticket

Lost and Found 失物招領

Useful Expressions 常用的表達方法

櫃檯人員

1. Nothing has been turned in today.

   今天沒有東西交過來。

2. I'll call you if a cell phone has been found.

   如果有手機被找到我會打電話給您。

3. There were two laptops turned in yesterday. You need to describe
   yours to me

   昨天有兩台手提電腦交過來。您需要跟我描述一下您的手提電腦。

Conversation 會話

(*Dana lost her **purse**. She goes to the Front Desk.*)

Dana: I lost my purse. Did someone **turn in** a purse yesterday? It's a black **clutch bag**.

Desk Clerk: There were two purses turned in yesterday. You need to **describe** your purse to me.

Dana: I had my credit cards, **cash**, **passport** and a **photo** inside. Everything should be under my name, Dana Young. It is a black **leather** clutch about the size of a small book.

Desk Clerk: Is this your purse?

Dana: Yes. That is my purse.

Desk Clerk: Here is your purse.

（唐娜遺失了她的錢包。她前往櫃檯。）

唐娜：我的錢包不見了。昨天有人拿來歸還嗎？它是一個黑色的女用手提包。

櫃檯人員：昨天有兩個錢包交到這裡。您必須向我描述一下您的錢包。

唐娜：錢包裡有我的信用卡，現金，護照以及照片。每樣東西上面應該都寫著我的名字，唐娜‧楊。它是皮製的提包，大小跟一本小的書差不多。

櫃檯人員：這個是您的手提包嗎？

唐娜：沒錯，那是我的手提包。

櫃檯人員：給您。

Word Bank 重要單字片語

1. purse [pɝs] n. 錢包；（女用）手提包

2. turn in v. phr. 交上；歸還

3. clutch bag [klʌtʃ bæg] n. 女用無帶提包

4. describe [dɪ`skraɪb] v. 描述

5. cash [kæʃ] n. 現金

6. passport [`pæs,pɔrt] n. 護照

7. photo [`foto] n. 照片

8. leather [`lɛðɚ] n. 皮革製品

Quiz 小試身手：請寫出正確英文單字

Guest: I lost my cell phone. Did someone t_____ i_____（繳交）a cell phone today?.

Desk Clerk: There were two. You need to d_____（描述）your purse to me.

Guest: It's a new i-phone.

答案：turn, in, describe

Extension 延伸學習：客房服務

接到電話時的問候

1. Good morning/afternoon/evening, room service.

   早安／午安／晚安，客房服務。

2. Room service. May I help you?

   客房服務。有需要幫忙的地方嗎？

回答客人可能的問題

1. Breakfast is available from 6:00 a.m. to 10:30 a.m.

   早餐在早上六點到十點半供應。

2. You'll find the menu for room service in the stationery folder in your room.

   你將可以在房間的文件夾找到客房服務的菜單。

詢問房號

May I have your room number, please? 請問你的房號？

關於上菜的時間

1. At what time shall we serve it?

   我們方便什麼時候上菜？

2. I'll have your breakfast sent up to you as soon as possible, sir.

   先生，我會盡快將您的早餐送上來。

3. It should take about twenty minutes, sir.

   先生，大約要花二十分鐘。

4. Your order should be there in about fifteen minutes.

   您的餐點將在大約十五分鐘後送來。

要進房間之前

This is room service. May I come in?

這是客房服務。我可以進來嗎？

詢問餐點 / 餐車 / 托盤該放哪

1. May I place the trolley/tray/cart here?

   我可以把餐車 / 托盤 / 手推車放這嗎？

2. Where should I put the trolley/tray/cart?

   我該把餐車 / 托盤 / 手推車放哪？

3. Where shall I set it?

   我該把餐點放置在哪？

餐車／托盤的處置

1. When you are finished, could you leave the tray in the hallway, please?

   當您用餐完畢時，可以請您將托盤放在走廊嗎？

2. We'll send someone to collect your trolley/tray.

   我們會派人來收餐車／托盤。

3. You may leave the trolley/tray on the hallway.

   你可以將餐車／托盤放在走廊。

詢問可否移動東西

1. May I move these bottles of beer aside?

   我可以把這幾罐啤酒移開嗎？

2. May I put these bottles of beer on the dressing table?

   我可以把這幾罐啤酒放在梳妝台嗎？

情境會話一

(*After a guest is calling for Room Service...*)

Room Service: Room Service. May I help you?

Guest: Yes. I would like to order lunch.

Room Service: Certainly, sir. May I take your order, please?

Guest: Yes, I'd like Beef Curry Rice, a salad and some beer.

Room Service: Certainly, sir. Which brand of beer do you prefer?

Guest: Taiwan beer.

Room Service: How many bottles would you like?

Guest: Two, please.

Room Service: How many glasses will you need?

Guest: Just one.

Room Service: I see. Will that be all?

Guest: Yes.

Room Service: Thank you, sir. Your order should be ready in about twenty minutes.

Guest: Fine. Thank you.

（在一個客人打電話要求客房服務之後…）

客房服務部：客房服務部，有需要幫忙的地方嗎？

客人：是的，我想點午餐。

客房服務部：好的，先生。現在可以點餐了嗎？

客人：是的，我要咖哩牛肉飯、沙拉以及啤酒。

客房服務部：好的，先生。您想要哪一個品牌的啤酒呢？

客人：台灣啤酒。

客房服務部：您想要幾罐呢？

客人：兩罐，謝謝。

客房服務部：您需要幾個杯子呢？

客人：只要一個。

客房服務部：我了解。這就是全部了嗎？

客人：是的。

客房服務部：謝謝您，先生。您的餐點將在大約二十分鐘後送達。

客人：很好，謝謝你。

情境會話二

（*When serving food in the room...*）

Waiter: This is Room Service. May I come in?

Guest: Yes, Please.

Waiter: Here is the food you ordered. Where shall I place the tray?

Guest: Please set it over there.

Waiter: Could you sign here, please?

Guest: Sure.

Waiter: Thank you, sir. When you have finished, and wish to have your tray removed, please dial number 9 for room service.

Guest: Yes, of course.

Waiter: Thank you, sir. Please enjoy your meal.

（當在房間裡上菜時…）

服務生：客房服務，我可以進來嗎？

客人：是的，請進。

服務生：這是您點的食物。我該把托盤放在哪裡？

客人：請放在這裡。

服務生： 可以請你在這簽名嗎？

客人：當然可以。

服務生：謝謝您，先生。當您用餐完畢，想要人來收時，請打分機9
　　　　找客房服務。

客人：好。

服務生：謝謝您，先生。祝用餐愉快。

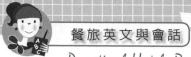
Multiple Choice 單一選擇題

1. Do you prefer a room with_____ view or mountain view?

    (A) service (B)ocean (C) jean (D) double

2. Is there a hotel _____ to the airport?

    (A) clerk (B) room (C) shuttle (D) breakfast

3. I have to do my _____, or I won't have pants to wear tomorrow.

    (A) call (B) form (C) laundry (D) drawer

4. May I have these trousers _____?

    (A) pressed (B) washing(C) dry (B) disturb

5. Would you please fill in the _____ card?

    (A) wake-up (B) key (C) faucet (D) registration

6. Please wash the sweater by hands, or it will _____.

    (A) shake (B) shrink (C) deliver (D) share

7. The package will be _____ tomorrow.

    (A) reserved (B) cleaned (C) delivered (D) ordered

8. What's the _____ of sending airmail?

    (A) maintenance (B) procedure (C) shuttle (D) dispatch

9. The fruit is _____. It's free.

    (A) complimentary (B) charged (C) satisfactory (D) postal

10. We'll have to get up early tomorrow morning. Do we need a
    _____ call?

    (A) emergency (B) phone (C) wake-up (D) lost

11. Valet: Good morning, ma'am. May I help you?

    Jane: Yes. _____

    Valet: This is your claim ticket. Please bring it with you when you
          leave.

    (A) Here is your room.

    (B) Here is your car.

    (C) Here is the key.

    (D) It's my pleasure.

12. Jane: _____

    Receptionist: It is served in the lobby between 7 and 9 am.

    (A) What time is it?

    (B) When will the dish be ready?

    (C) When will the mail arrive in Taipei?

    (D) When will breakfast be offered?

13. Jane: I lost my purse. Did someone turn in a purse yesterday?

    Desk Clerk: _____.

    Jane: It's a black bag, with my credit cards, cash and passport
          inside.

    (A) Could you do me a favor?

    (B) Would you like to have a drink?

(C) Could you please give me a brief description about your purse to me?

(D) Do you want to buy a new purse?

14. Receptionist: _____

    Jane: Jane Hunt.

    (A) Did you make a reservation?

    (B) How are you doing?

    (C) What name is the reservation under?

    (D) Where are you from?

15. Receptionist: Hello, can I help you?

    Jane: Yes,_____

    (A) I'll be right back with your order.

    (B) I need a wake up call at 7:30 tomorrow morning.

    (C) I'm Jane Hunt.

    (D) I'll send someone immediately

16. Jane: Good morning. _____

    Desk Clerk: I'll call a taxi dispatch for you. May I have your name,

    please?

    (A) I need a cab to take me to the airport.

    (B) Dana Young.

    (C) I need a wake up call at 6:30

    (D) I would like to order something to eat.

17. Desk Clerk: Good evening, Ma'am._____

    Jane: Yes. My name is Dana Young.

    Desk Clerk: Ms. Young. You reserved a double room with a

    mountain view.

    (A) Do you have a credit card?

    (B) Can you help me?

    (C) Would you like to have a single room?

    (D) Do you have a reservation with us?

18. Jane: What are your rates?

    Clerk: _____

    Jane: Oh, I see.

    (A) It's 6: 40.

    (B) That rate chart is on your television, ma'am.

    (C) The laundry will be delivered to your room at 7:30.

    (D) They are fine and delicious.

19. Housekeeper: Housekeeping. May I come in?

    Jane: Yes, _____

    Housekeeper: Certainly, ma'am.

    (A) I need a wake-up call.

    (B) I need a taxi.

    (C) I want have this laundry done.

    (D) I need a ride to the airport.

20. Housekeeper: Would you please fill out the laundry form first?

Jane: Sure. _____

Housekeeper: Certainly, ma'am. Here you are.

(A) May I come in?

(B) May I use your pen?

(C) May I have your name?

(D) May I take the order?

答案： (B)(C)(C)(A)(D)(B)(C)(B)(A)(C)

(C)(D)(C)(C)(B)(A)(D)(B)(C)(B)

Telephone Conversation

5 電話對話

 本章摘要

Telephone Manner 電話禮貌

Telephone Number 電話號碼的說明

Transferring or Connecting 轉接給客人或客房

Taking Telephone Messages 留話給客人

International Calls 國際電話的使用說明

Extension 延伸學習

Introduction 學習重點

　　在電話中用英文對話，比面對面溝通更加困難，因為沒有了眼神、嘴形及肢體語言的輔助。如何在電話中精準的掌握對方語言，顯得更為重要。電話禮儀也是飯店或是餐廳建立專業服務、給客人好的第一印象的關鍵。旅館的總機人員，必須能及時解答客人電話中的各種詢問、立即處理或轉接正確的房間或單位，接電話的禮貌、語氣及效率是三大重點。在本單元，我們將會學到一些實用的電話相關字詞及用語，在電話禮貌、電話號碼的說明、轉接、留話以及國際電話的使用上，都能讓你有足夠的認識，以應付未來可能遇到的狀況。

Useful Words 常用字彙

電話用語相關字詞

answering machine	答錄機
call display	來電顯示
cellular phone cell phone mobile phone（英）	手機
directory phone book	電話簿
extension	分機
external line	外線
receiver	電話聽筒；受話器
dial tone	撥號音

busy signal	嗶一聲（表示忙線中）
operator	接線生
caller	打電話者
recipient/answerer	接電話者
phone	電話 (a telephone) 打電話 (v. telephone)
ring	鈴聲；鐘聲 按（鈴）；搖（鈴）(v.)
call back/phone back	回電話 (v.)
dial	撥（電話號碼）(v.)
pick up	接電話 (v.)
hang up	掛電話 (v.)

Telephone Manner 電話禮貌

Useful Expressions 常用的表達方法

1. 接電話的侍者，需用愉悅、清楚、抑揚頓挫合適的聲音說話。並且字句分明，母音及子音都需發音清楚。

2. 當接聽電話的時候，接電話的侍者需用"Good Morning" 或 "Good Afternoon" 先問候對方，然後說出飯店名稱。

3. 回答的時候需要有精神但又不能太做作，太做作會產生疏離感。

4. 一旦知道對方的名字之後，就用Mr / Mrs / Miss＋姓氏來稱呼對方。

5. 俚語及朋友之間的用語應避免使用，以下是需要避免的字詞。

應避免的字詞	正確說法
Hi, JM Hotel. What do you want?	Good morning, JM Hotel. May I help you?
OK	Certainly, Mr./Mrs./Miss _____.
It is very busy here. Call back later.	I'm sorry. The line is busy now. Would you like to call back later?
There is no Mr. Johnson here. Bye.	I'm afraid that Mr. Johnson is no longer staying at the hotel.
Hang on.	1. Will you hold the line, please? 2. One moment, please. 3. Could you hang up, please?
He/she's out	I am sorry but Mr./Mrs./Miss_____ is not in the office at the moment, can I take a message for you?
1. Mr. Who? 2. What's that you said? 3. What? I don't understand a word you're saying. 4. Speak louder. I can't hear you.	1. Could you repeat that please? 2. Would you say that again? 3. Could you speak more slowly, please? 4. I'm sorry. I think we had a bad connection. Could you please speak a little louder please?

Conversation 會話

(*A guest is calling the front desk.*)

Guest: Excuse me. There is something **wrong** with the television.

Clerk: I'll **ask** someone to check your room **as soon as possible**.

Guest: Thank you very much.

Clerk: It's my **pleasure**. I would like to apologize for the **inconvenience**.

（一個客人打電話到櫃檯。）

客人：不好意思。電視好像出了點問題。

櫃檯人員：我會請人盡快到您的房間看一下。

客人：非常感謝你。

櫃檯人員：這是我的榮幸。很抱歉對您造成不便。

Word Bank 重要單字片語

1. wrong [rɔŋ] adj. 錯誤的

2. ask [æsk] v. 要求；詢問

3. as soon as possible 盡快

4. pleasure [`plɛʒɚ] n. 愉快；樂趣

5. inconvenience [ˌɪnkən`vinjəns] n. 不便

Quiz 小試身手：請寫出正確英文單字

1. I'm sorry. I think we had a bad c_____（連結）. Could you please speak a little l_____ please?

2. Guest: Excuse me. There is something w_____ with the air-conditioner.

   Clerk: I'll ask someone to check your room as soon as p_____.

   Guest: Thank you very much.

   Clerk: It's my p_____. I would like to a_____（道歉）for

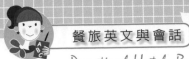
the i＿＿＿＿＿＿（不便）.

答案：connection, louder, wrong, possible, pleasure, apologize, inconvenience

Telephone Number 電話號碼的說明

Useful Expressions 常用的表達方法

I'm sorry but this line is not too clear.	我很抱歉通話不是太清楚。
May I know who you're trying to reach?	我可以知道您在試著聯絡哪位嗎？
Who would you like to speak to?	您想要跟那位說話呢？
If you want, we can place a call for you, sir.	如果您想要的話，我們可為您打電話。

Conversation 1 會話一

（*A caller wants to call his friend outside the hotel.*）

Operator: This is the Operator. May I help you?

Caller: Yes. I'd like to call my friends **outside** this hotel. What shall I do?

Operator: For calls inside Taipei, please dial 0 first, wait for the dial tone, and then dial the number you want to call. Dialing the area code of 02 is not **necessary**. If you want to, we can place a call for you, sir.

Caller: No, I think I'll try it myself, thanks. What about outside Taipei? I'd like to call Tao Yuan.

Operator: For calls outside Taipei, please dial 0, then the area code of 03 and the number.

Caller: I see, well, what about room to room calls? What shall I do?

Operator: Do you know your friend's room number, sir?

Caller: Yes, it's Room 85.

Operator: For room numbers with 2 **digits**, please dial 20 and then the room number.

Caller: Thank you very much.

Operator: You're welcome, sir.

（有人來電想打電話給飯店外的朋友。）

接線生：接線生。我可以為您效勞嗎？

來電者：是的。我想打電話給我飯店外的朋友。我該怎麼做？

接線生：如果是台北市內電話，請先播0，再等待撥號音，然後播打您
　　　　想要打的電話。　不必撥打區域號碼02。先生，如果您需要，
　　　　我可以幫您撥打。

來電者：不用，我想我可以自己試試看，謝謝。那如果是台北市以外
的地方呢？我想打到桃園。

接線生：如果是台北市以外，先撥0，然後區域號碼03，再來是您要打
的號碼。

來電者：我懂了。那在飯店內房間對房間的撥打方式呢？我該怎麼做
呢？

接線生：您知道您朋友的房號嗎，先生？

來電者：知道，85號房。

接線生：兩位數的房號，請先撥打20，再撥房間號碼。

來電者：非常感謝您。

接線生：不客氣，先生。

Word Bank 重要單字片語

1. outside [`aut`saɪd] prep. 在外面；向外面

2. necessary [`nɛsə‚sɛrɪ] adj. 必要的；必需的

3. digit [`dɪdʒɪt] n. 數字

Conversation 2 會話二

(*While an operator is calling for the guest...*)

Guest: I've tried calling a number in Tao Yuan but I can't understand what the other party was saying. Could you place the call for me?

Operator: Certainly, sir. I'd be glad to help you. What number are you calling, please?

Guest: 433-8251.

Operator: Is this a **company** number or a **resident** number?

Guest: A company one.

Operator: May I have the name of the company, please?

Guest: Yes, it's Huai Lin Publishing.

Operator: Who would you like to speak to, please?

Guest: Ms. Huang of the **Editing Department**.

Operator: Do you know her extension number or her **full** name?

Guest: Not the extension number but I think her name is Huang Huai-Yu.

Operator: May I have your name and room number, please?

Guest: Yes, my name is Nat and I'm in Room 983.Thank you.

（當接線生在幫客人打電話時⋯）

客人：我一直試著要打在桃園的一個電話，但我不了解對方在說什麼。可以請你幫我打嗎？

接線生：當然，先生。我很高興幫可以幫忙您。請問您在打哪個電話？

客人：433-8251。

接線生：這是公司的號碼還是住家的號碼？

客人：公司號碼。

接線生：請問我可以知道公司名稱嗎？

客人：可以，是懷凌出版社。

接線生：您想要跟誰說話呢？

客人：編輯部的黃女士。

接線生：您知道她的分機或是全名嗎？

客人：我不知道分機但我想她的名字是黃懷玉。

接線生：請問您的名字及房號？

客人：可以，我的名字是納特，我在983號房。謝謝你。

Word Bank 重要單字片語

1. company [ˋkʌmpənɪ] n. 公司

2. resident [ˋrɛzədənt] n. 居民；定居者

3. edit [ˋɛdɪt] v. 編輯；校訂

4. department [dɪˋpartmənt] n.（企業等的）部門

5. full [ful] adj. 完全的；完整的

Quiz 小試身手：請寫出正確英文單字

1. Caller: I'd like to call my friends outside this hotel. What shall I do?

   Operator: For calls inside Taipei, please d_____（撥號）0 first, wait for the dial tone, and then dial the number you want to call. Dialing the a_____ c_____（區域號碼）of 02 is not n_____（必要的）. If you want, we can p_____ a call for you, sir.

2. O_____（接線生）: Certainly, sir. I'd be glad to help you. What number are you calling, please?

   Guest: 2219-2700.

   Operator: Is this a c_____（公司）number or a r_____（住家）number?

答案：dial, area code, necessary, place, Operator, company, resident

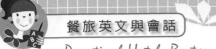
Transferring or Connecting 轉接給客人或客房

Useful Expressions 常用的表達方法

1. I'll connect you with/to _____(e.g. the Reservation Desk).

   我將為您轉接到_____（預約櫃檯）。

2. I'm afraid S（主詞）+V（動詞）...

   例句：

   (1) I'm afraid you have the wrong number. 恐怕你打錯電話了。

   (2) I'm afraid the line is bad/ busy. 恐怕線路不好 / 忙碌。

   (3) I'm afraid we have no room with that number, sir. 恐怕我們沒有這個房號，先生。

   (4) I'm afraid there's no guest with that name. 恐怕我們沒有這個客人。

   (5) I'm afraid there is no reply/answer. 恐怕沒有回應。

Conversation 1 會話一

（*A guest is calling his friend inside JK Hotel.*）

Guest: Is this the JK Hotel?

Operator: Speaking. May I help you?

Guest: Yes. Could you put me through to Room 1235, please?

Operator: **Certainly**, sir. Just a moment, please.

（一個客人正打電話找住在JK旅館的朋友。）

客人：這是JK飯店嗎？

接線生：是的。我可以為您效勞嗎？

客人：是的。可以請你幫我接到1235房嗎？

接線生：當然，先生。請稍待片刻。

Word Bank 重要單字片語

1. certainly [ˋsɝtənlɪ] adv.（用於回答）當然；可以；沒問題

Conversation 2 會話二

Operator: Who would you like to speak to?

Guest: I'd like to speak with Mr. Johnson.

Operator: Is he a hotel guest here, sir?

Guest: Yes.

Operator: Will you hold the line, please? I'll check for you.

   Thank you for waiting, sir. I'll **connect** you to Room 926.

接線生：請問您想要跟誰說話？

客人：我想跟強森先生說話。

接線生：他是飯店的房客嗎，先生？

客人：是的。

接線生：請稍待片刻。我將幫您確認。感謝您的等候，先生。

   我將為您轉接到926號房。

Word Bank 重要單字片語

1. connect [kə`nɛkt] v. 給…接通電話[(+with)]

Quiz 小試身手：請寫出正確英文單字

Guest: Is this the Moon Hotel?

Operator: S_____g. May I help you?

Guest: Yes. Could you put me t_____ to Room 108, please?

Operator: C_____, sir. Just a m_____t, please.

答案：Speaking, through, Certainly, moment

Taking Telephone Messages 留話給客人

Useful Expressions 常用的表達方法

接線生

Thank you for waiting/patience.	謝謝您的等待／耐心。
I'm afraid there's no reply/answer.	恐怕沒有回應／回答。
May/Can I take a message for you?	我可以為您留言嗎？

留言給客人的紙條應包括

the name of the person for whom the message is intended	留話給誰
the name of the person leaving the message and the company	留話者
his / her telephone number	留話者的電話號碼
the nature of the message (urgency and how delivered)	此訊息的性質（急迫性及如何傳遞的）
whether the caller will ring or call back	來電者是否會再打來
a summary of the message giving special attention to figures	訊息摘要，特別注意數字訊息
date the message was received	日期
time the message was received	時間
signature or initials of person taking the message	幫忙留話者

Conversation 1 會話一

(*while there is no reply*...)

Caller: Hello. May I speak to Mr. York in Room 1235, please?

Operator: Certainly, sir. Just a moment, please.

(*After a while*...)

Operator: Thank you for waiting, sir. I'm afraid there's no reply.

Caller: Could you try again?

Operator: Of course, sir. Just a moment, please.

(*After a while*...)

Operator: Thank your for you patience. I'm afraid there's still no answer.

Caller: Then can I leave a **message** for him?

Operator: Sure, sir. I'll **transfer** you to the Message Desk.

（當沒有回應的時候…）
來電者：喂，請問我可以跟1235號房的約克先生說話嗎？
接線生：當然，先生。請稍待片刻。
（過了一會兒…）
接線生：先生，謝謝您的等待。恐怕沒人回應。
來電者：你可以再試一次嗎？
接線生：當然可以，先生。請稍待片刻。
（又過了一會兒…）
接線生：先生，謝謝您的耐心。恐怕還是沒人回應。
來電者：那我可以留言給他嗎？
接線生：當然，先生。我將為您轉接到留言櫃檯。

Word Bank 重要單字片語

1. message [ˋmɛsɪdʒ] n. 訊息
2. transfer [trænsˋfɝ] v. 轉接

Conversation 2 會話二

(*while taking a telephone message*...)

Waitress: We're sorry to have kept you waiting. We've paged Mr. Wang but there was no answer. I'm afraid he is not here at the moment.

Caller: He should be there. Could you give him a message when he arrives?

Waitress: Certainly, sir. Go ahead, please.

Caller: **I was supposed to** have dinner with him but I will be late.

Could you tell him that I'll meet him in the business center at 7:30?

Waitress: I got it. May I have your name, please?

Caller: Yes. It's Gordon.

Waitress: Mr. Gordon, does Mr. Wang have your number?

Caller: I think so, but I'd better leave it again **just in case.**

Waitress: May I have the number, please?

Caller: It's 236-7086.

Waitress: Thank you. I'll pass the message to Mr. Wang.

Caller: **It's very kind of you.** Thank you.

Waitress: Sure. It's my pleasure.

（留電話訊息時…）

女服務生：讓您等待我們感到很抱歉。我們已經呼叫王先生，但沒有
回應。恐怕他此刻不在這裡。

來電者：他應該在這的。你可以在他到的時候，給他我的留言嗎？

女服務生：先生，當然可以。請說。

來電者：我預定要跟他一起用晚餐，但我會遲到。可以請你告訴他我
將會在七點半在商務中心與他見面嗎？

女服務生：我知道了，請問您大名？

來電者：我叫戈登。

女服務生：戈登先生，王先生有您的電話嗎？

來電者：我想應該有。不過我最好還是再留一次，以防萬一。

女服務生：可以告訴我電話號碼嗎？

來電者：236-7086.

女服務生：謝謝您。我將會轉告王先生。

來電者：你人真好。謝謝你。

女服務生：應該的。這是我的榮幸。

Word Bank 重要單字片語

1. be supposed to + 原形動詞 應該

2. just in case 以防萬一

3. It's very kind of you. 你人真好

Conversation 3 會話三

(*while giving the message*...)

Guest: Excuse me. I'm **expecting** a friend but he hasn't arrived.

　　　Did he leave a message for me?

Waitress: May I have your name, please?

Guest: It's Wang.

Waitress: May I have your friend's name, please?

Guest: It's Gordon.

Waitress: Please wait a second. I'll check for you.

(*After a few seconds*...)

Waitress: Excuse me, sir. Mr. Gordon called fifteen minutes ago to

　　　　ask you to meet him in the business center at 7:30. His

　　　　number is 236-7086.

Guest: I see. Thank you.

Waitress: You're welcome.

（留言的時候…）

客人：不好意思，我正在等一個朋友，但他還沒來。他有留言給我嗎？

女服務生：請問您的名字是？

客人：王。

女服務生：請問您的朋友的名字是？

客人：戈登。

女服務生：請稍待片刻，我將為您確認。

（幾秒鐘之後…）

女服務生：不好意思，先生。戈登先生十五分鐘前有打來，請你七點半在商務中心與他見面。他的電話是236-7086。

客人：我知道了。謝謝你。

女服務生：不客氣。

Word Bank 重要單字片語

1. expect [ɪk`spɛkt] v. 期待；等待；盼望

Quiz 小試身手：請寫出正確英文單字

1. Operator: Just a moment, please.

   (*After a while...*)

   Operator: Thank you for you p_____（耐心）. I'm a_____ there's s_____ no a_____.（恐怕仍然沒有回應。）

   Caller: Then can I l_____ a m_____ for him?（我可以留言給他嗎）

2. Caller: He should be there. Could you give him a message when

　　　he a＿＿＿＿＿（抵達）?

　Waitress: Certainly, sir. G＿＿＿ a＿＿＿, please（請說）.

答案：patience, afraid, still, answer, leave, message, arrives, Go, ahead

International Calls 國際電話的使用說明

Useful Expressions 常用的表達方法

a domestic call	國內電話
an international call/overseas call	國際電話 / 海外電話
long-distance call	長途電話
a local call	市內電話
counter call	對方付費電話（公共電話時使用）
paid call	已付費電話
directory assistance	查號台

Conversation 會話

（*A caller wants to make an international call.*）

Caller: Hi, I'd like to make an **international**/overseas call to Taiwan.

Operator: Just a moment, please.

(*After a while*...)

Operator: What number are you calling?

Caller: It's 272-1058, the area code is 02.

Operator: Hang on and wait, please. I'll **inform** you when I've put the call through.

(*After a while*...)

Operator: Will that be all, ma'am?

Caller: Yes.

Operator: That's six dollars and thirty cents.

(有人想要打國際電話。)

來電者：我想打國際電話到台灣。

接線生： 請稍後。

（一會兒之後…）

接線生： 請問您要打的電話是？

來電者： 272-1058，區域號碼是02。

接線生：請不要掛斷，稍待一下。當我將您轉接之後，我會讓您知道。

（一會兒之後…）

接線生：這樣就可以了嗎，女士？

來電者：是的。

接線生：通話費一共是六美元三十分。

Word Bank 重要單字片語

1. international [ˌɪntəˈnæʃənḷ] adj. 國際性的；國際間的
2. inform [ɪnˈfɔrm] v. 通知；告知；報告

Quiz 小試身手：請寫出正確英文單字

Caller: I'd like to make an i_____ (=overseas) call to Hong Kong.

Operator: Just a moment, please.

(*After a while*…)

Operator: What number are you calling?

Caller: 2218-1000, the a_____ c_____ is 02.

Operator: H_____ on and wait, please. I'll i_____ you know when I've p_____ the call through.

答案：international, area, code, Hang, inform, put

大哉問：國際電話的撥打，需要透過接線生嗎？

本來國際電話都需要經接線生接線。自國際直接撥號（IDD）於1970年代發明後，撥打國際電話可以不用經接線生，但僅限於主要城市。

方式：當地國際冠碼 ＋ 收話者的國碼 ＋ 區域號碼（去0）＋ 收話者電話號碼。

例如：由日本打到台灣：
先撥日本國際冠碼 001 後，撥台灣國碼 886，
再撥台北區域號碼 2（去掉0），最後撥對方號碼。

Extension 延伸學習：電話用語的秘訣

1. Speak slowly and clearly.
   由於不是以母語溝通，所以在說話的時候盡可能慢慢說，且發音清楚，以便他人了解。

2. Make sure you understand the other speaker.
   要確定你聽懂了。尤其是在幫客人轉達訊息時，要能不害怕再次確認，或是要求重述，以確保訊息的正確性。

3. Practice with a friend.
   找時間跟朋友進行角色扮演的練習，要注意不能看到對方的嘴唇，以模擬真實電話對話的情形。

4. Use businesses and recordings.
   可試著播打一些免費服務電話，能以英文詢問，提出你的要求，記得隨身要有紙筆，並向對方確認你的理解是否正確。

5. Learn telephone etiquette (manners).
   要學習電話禮儀，我們不是以英文為母語的人，常常不懂得用一些情態助動詞如 "could" 或 "may"，如能熟悉怎麼用正式的語言，有禮貌的應對，也是重要課題。

6. Practice dates and numbers.
   如第一章所介紹，我們必須熟悉怎麼用英文快速的聽及說數字，可以多練習用英文講出日期或是數字。

Multiple Choice 單一選擇題

1. I will _____ you when I put you through.

   (A) know (B) inform (C) specify (D) bother

2. Please _____ on a minute. I'll be right back.

   (A) come (B) hold (C) inform (D) wait

3. If you want to eat at that restaurant, you'd better make a(n) _____ first.

   (A) reservation (B) message (C) interview (D) calls

4. Do you have any _____ appointment today?

   (A) overdone (B) scheduled (C) canceled (D) medium

5. _____on, please.

   (A) Wait (B) Put (C) Hang (D) Check

6. Your friend leave a _____ to you. He will be twenty minutes late.

   (A) seat (B) speaker (C) extension (D) message

7. Bob: I am looking for a Frank Thomas. Can you tell me if he is here?

   Waiter: _____

   Bob: Thank you.

   (A) Thank you for your patience.

   (B) You're welcome.

   (C) You are unexpected, sir.

(D) Wait for a minute, please.

8. Jack: Hi, this is Jack. Is Tom in?

   Tom's mother: Yes. _____

   (A) Please try calling later.

   (B) I'm Jack.

   (C) Hold on a minute.

   (D) Thank you for your time.

9. Waiter: _____ May I help you?

   Candy: Yes. I am trying to contact to Mr. Johnson.

   (A) Hang up, please.

   (B) Jackson's Thai Cuisine. This is Tommy.

   (C) Please go this way.

   (D) Just answer me, sir.

10. Secretary: I'm sorry, ma'am. Mr Lin is not here now. _____

    Jane: Yes. This is her friend, Jane. Please tell her that I need to cancel the meeting tonight.

    (A) Can I leave a message to her?

    (B) I'll inform her that you've called her.

    (C) Would you like to leave a message?

    (D) Could you call her at 0900-000-123?

11. Waiter: Hello, Jerry's Café. This is Judy. _____

    April: Yes. I'd like to make a reservation for four people at 6:30.

    (A) Could you do me a favor?

(B) Are you looking for a Mr. Lu?

(C) Can I help you?

(D) Would you like to order something?

12. Operator: Mr. Jackson, we have a message for you. Your friend
Pete said that he couldn't come here on time, and he'll
be here as soon as possible .

Mr. Jackson: I see. _____

(A) Thank you for giving him the chance.

(B) Thank you for calling him.

(C) Thank you for taking the message for me.

(C) Thank you for calling for me.

13. Sherry: I am looking for Dan Robinson.

Operator: I'm sorry. _____

(A) I'll give him the message.

(B) Are you through?

(C) Sure. Go ahead.

(D) Nobody by that name works here.

14. John: Good morning. John speaking.

Joanna: Hi, John. This is Joanna. I'd like to speak to Mr. Li.

John: Oh, he is not here at the moment.

Joanna: Could you give him a message for me?

John: _____

Joanna: Please tell him that I will visit him on Sunday afternoon.

(A) I'm not sure whether he will be free or not.

(B) I'm sorry. I can't.

(C) Of course. Go ahead.

(D) Can you say that again?

15. David: Could you tell me if there is a customer there by the name of James Wang?

Waiter: _____

David: Thank you.

(A) This is Jim. Can I help you?

(B) You have the wrong number.

(C) Would you like to leave a message?

(D) One moment, please. I'll check.

16. Rita: Could you tell me if there is a customer there by the name of Jerry Lin?

Waiter: Please hold on a minute.

(*After a few minutes*)

Waiter: I'm sorry, sir. _____

Rita: Thank you.

(A) I will give Mr. Lin the message.

(B) We tried to page Mr. Lin but there is no answer.

(C) I'd like to speak to the manager.

(D) He'll be here soon.

17. Jane: Hello. I'd like to speak to Mr. Johnson.

    Jerry: _____

    Jane: Could you give him a message?

    (A) Hang on, please.

    (B) He is on vacation. .

    (C) I'll tell him that he has an appointment with you.

    (D) OK. I'll put you through.

18. Waiter: Could I have your phone number please?

    Amy: OK. 7500-8800.

    Waiter: Is that 7500-8900?

    Amy: _____

    (A) No, 8600.

    (B) No, 8800.

    (C) No, 6550-8800.

    (D) Yes, it's correct.

19. Guest: Is this the Joon Hotel?

    Operator: Speaking. Can I help you?

    Guest: Yes. _____

    Operator: Certainly, sir. A moment, please.

    (A) Would you like to leave a meesage?

    (B) Could you repeat that message?

    (C) May I have your friend's name?

    (D) Could you put me through to Room 1285, please?

20. Operator: What number are you calling, please?

Guest: 436-7856.

Operator: _____

Guest: A company one.

(A) Is it correct?

(B) Is this a company number or a resident number?

(C) Are you sure?

(D) Could you please say that again?

答案： (B)(B)(A)(B)(C)(D)(D)(C)(B)(C)

(C)(C)(D)(C)(D)(B)(B)(B)(D)(B)

Meeting and Receiving Guests in a Restaurant

6 餐廳迎接客人

 本章摘要

Welcoming Guests 歡迎客人的光臨

Getting Seated 帶位與領檯

No Seats Available 客滿及等候客人之招呼

Extension 延伸學習

Introduction 學習重點

　　在餐廳的服務當中，帶位人員的態度及反應，表現是否合宜，是給客人對餐廳的整體印象的第一道關卡，也通常是最重要的一部分。本章將介紹帶位與領檯時、招呼客人時、客滿時及對等候客人的招呼時、以及點酒時，如何用英文順暢的溝通及處理。

Useful Words 常用字彙

基本用字

menu	菜單
bill	帳單
smoking section/area	吸煙區
nonsmoking section/area	禁煙區
serving trolley	小餐車
tray	托盤

工作人員

valet	泊車服務生
chef	主廚
host/hostess	領檯：帶位的先生 / 帶位的小姐
waiter/waitress	男服務生 / 女服務生
bar manager	吧台經理

bartender	酒保
manager	經理
busboy	外場小弟
cashier	出納／收銀員
counter	櫃檯

Welcoming Guests 歡迎客人的光臨

Useful Expressions 常用的表達方法

問候

Good afternoon, welcome to ＿＿＿＿＿＿（餐廳名稱）.

是否有預約

1. Do you have a reservation?

   請問有預約嗎？

2. If yes, let me show you to your table.

   如果有，請讓我帶位。

3. If no, please wait a moment. I'll check to see if we have a table available.

   如果沒有，請稍待片刻。我為您確認我們是否有空位。

問人數

1. How many people?

   多少人？

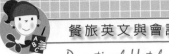

2. Party of four?

四個人一起嗎？

3. Table for two?

雙人桌嗎？

位置的安排

1. Smoking or non-smoking?

吸煙區或是非吸煙區？

2. Would you like a table in the smoking or non-smoking section?

你想要吸煙區的還是非吸煙區的座位？

3. Would you like a window seat?

你想要靠窗的位置嗎？

帶位

1. Please follow me.

請跟我來。

2. Please come this way.

請往這個方向。

3. Here's your table. Enjoy your meal.

這是您的座位。祝用餐愉快。

Conversation 會話

(*A waiter is talking to a guest.*)

Host: Hi, I'm Nat. I will be your waiter for today. How are you today?

Guest: Pretty good, thanks.

Host: Do you have a reservation?

Guest: Yes, we do.

Host: Under what name was the table **reserved**?

Guest: Smith.

Host: How many in your party?

Guest: Four.

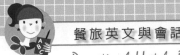
Host: Smoking or non-smoking?

Guest: Non-smoking, please.

Host: This way, please. You'll be **seated** at table 5, near a window.

Guest: Thank you.

（服務生正和客人對話）

領檯：嗨，我是納特，您今天的服務生。您好嗎？

客人：很好，謝謝。

領檯：您有預約嗎？

客人：有的。

領檯：是用哪個名字訂位的？

客人：史密斯。

領檯：您們一共幾個人？

客人：四個。

領檯：吸煙區或是非吸煙區？

客人：非吸煙區，謝謝。

領檯：請往這個方向。您們坐在靠近窗戶的第五桌。

客人：謝謝。

Word Bank 重要單字片語

1. reserved [rɪˋzɝvd] adj. 留做專用的；預訂的
2. seated [sitɪd] adj. 就座的；有…座位的

Quiz 小試身手：請寫出正確英文單字

Host: Good evening. Do you have a r_____?

Gary: Yes, I've booked a table f_____ two. The name is Smith.

Host: Let me see... Ah, yes, Mr. Smith. Your table will be r_____
in about five minutes.

Gary: Thank you.

Host: Mr. Gary, your table is ready. Please come this w_____.

答案：reservation, for, ready, come, way

Getting Seated 帶位與領檯

Useful Expressions 常用的表達方法

1. Do you have a reservation?
   請問您有預約訂位嗎？

2. Please come this way.
   請往這邊走。

3. Please, follow me.
   請跟我來。

4. Is this table satisfactory?
   這個座位還滿意嗎？

Conversation 會話

(*A host is getting a guest seated.*)

Host: Good evening, do you have a reservation?

Guest: Yes, Linda Hsieh.

Host: Please follow me, Miss Hsieh.

(*After a few seconds...*)

Host: Is this table **satisfactory**?

Guest: The table is too close to the restroom, could we have another one?

Host: Would you **mind** sitting at a table by the dance floor?

Guest: No. A table in the corner would be fine.

Host: Please come this way.

(*After a few seconds*...)

Host: Please have a seat.

Guest: Thanks.

Host: A waiter will come to take your order in just a minute.

（領檯正在帶領客人就坐。）

領檯：晚安，請問您有預約訂位嗎？

客人：有的，琳達‧謝。

領檯：請跟我來，謝小姐。

（幾秒鐘之後…）

領檯：這個座位還滿意嗎？

客人：這個座位太靠近廁所，我們可以換一個嗎？

領檯：您介意坐在舞池旁的位子嗎？

客人：不介意。在角落的位子不錯。

領檯：請往這個方向。

（幾秒鐘之後…）

領檯：請坐。

客人：謝謝。

領檯：一分鐘之後服務生會來為您點餐。

Word Bank 重要單字片語

1. satisfactory [ˌsætɪsˋfæktərɪ] adj. 令人滿意的；符合要求的

2. mind [maɪnd] v. （用於否定句和疑問句中）介意；反對 +V-ing

Quiz 小試身手

配合題（請選適當的回答）

Guest:	Host:
1.We don't smoke.	a. No problem. I'll move one of the chairs out of the way.
2.My wife has a wheelchair. Can you accommodate her?	b. No problem. I'll seat you in the non-smoking section.
3.We'd like a table by the window, if possible.	c. No problem. I'll show them to your table.
4.We've got three kids with us. Do you have high-chairs?	d. No problem. I'll clear one for you right away.
5.My mother has a hearing problem. Do you have a quiet table?	e. No problem. I'll arrange a table for you in the corner.
6.I'm meeting some friends later. Could you please let them know I'm here?	f. No problem. I'll borrow one from the coffee shop next door.

答案：1. b 2. a 3. d. 4. f. 5. e. 6. c.

No Seats Available 客滿及等候客人之招呼

Useful Expressions 常用的表達方法

抱歉，我們已客滿

1. Sorry, we have no free tables (available) now.

   抱歉，我們已經沒有位子了。

2. Sorry, we're fully booked.

   抱歉，我們已經被訂滿了。

3. Sorry, we're full at the moment.

   抱歉，現在我們客滿了。

抱歉，讓您久等

1. Thank you for waiting.

   謝謝您的等待。

2. Sorry for the delay.

   抱歉，耽誤了一下。

我馬上就來

1. I'll be with you shortly.

   我馬上就來。

2. I'll be right with you.

   我馬上就來。

3. One moment, please.

   請稍待片刻。

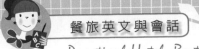
Conversation 1 會話一

(*A hostess is politely asking the guests to wait for a while.*)

Hostess: Good afternoon. How many are there in your party?

Guest: There are four of us.

Hostess: I have a table in the smoking section, if that's OK.

Guest: You don't have anything available in the non-smoking section?

Hostess: I'm afraid not. It's about a ten-minute wait.

Guest: That's OK, we'll wait.

Hostess: May I have your name, please?

Guest: It's Nicole.

Hostess: OK, Ms. Nicole. Please have a seat here. We'll call you as soon as a table is available.

(*After a while*...)

Hostess: Ms. Nicole? We're sorry to have kept you waiting. Your table is **ready** now. Please come this way.

（領檯人員禮貌的要求客人稍待片刻。）

領檯：午安。請問你們一共幾個人？

客人：我們有四個人。

領檯：在吸煙區有個座位，如果可以的話。

客人：在非吸煙區沒有位子了嗎？

領檯：恐怕沒有。大約要等十分鐘。

客人：沒關係，我們等。

領檯：請問您的名字是？

客人：妮可。

領檯：好的，妮可小姐。請坐。我們一有位子會馬上通知您。

（一會兒之後）

領檯：妮可小姐？很抱歉讓您等候。您的座位已經準備好了。請往這
　　　個方向走。

Word Bank 重要單字片語

1. ready [ˋrɛdɪ] adj. 準備好的

Conversation 2 會話二

（*There aren't any table available in this restaurant now.*）

Host: Hello, how are you this evening?

Guest: I'm fine, thank you.

Host: I'm sorry. There is no **vacancy** just now. Could you please
　　　wait for a while?

Guest: How long do we have to wait?

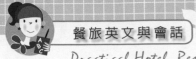
Host: It'll be just a few minutes. Would you like to order something to drink first?

Guest: Sure. I'll have a beer.

（現在沒有空的位子。）

領檯：哈囉，今晚好嗎？

客人：我很好，謝謝你。

領檯：我很抱歉。現在沒有空位。可以請您稍待一下嗎？

客人：我們必須等多久？

領檯：大約只要幾分鐘。你想要先點個東西喝嗎？

客人：好啊。我要啤酒。

Word Bank 重要單字片語

1. vacancy [`vekənsɪ] n. 空桌；空房

Quiz 小試身手：請寫出正確英文單字

1.Sorry, we have no v_____ (=free tables available) now.

2.Sorry for the d_____.（抱歉，耽誤了一下。）

3.It's about five-m_____ wait.（大約要等五分鐘）

答案：vacancy, delay, minute

 Extension 延伸學習：點酒

酒的種類

ale	麥酒
beer	啤酒 imported/local beer 進口／本地啤酒
brandy	白蘭地
cognac	干邑白蘭地
dark beer	黑啤酒
draft beer	生啤酒
light beer	淡啤酒
red wine	紅酒
spirits	烈酒
whiskey	威士忌 1. Scotch 蘇格蘭威士忌 2. Bourbon 波本威士忌（美產） 3. Canadian Whiskey 加拿大威士忌 4. Irish Whiskey 愛爾蘭威士忌
white wine	白酒

wine	葡萄酒 1. 產地 　(1)Bordeaux 波爾多（法） 　(2)Napa valley （美） 　(3)Burgundy 勃根地（法） 　(4)The Cotes du Rhone隆河谷地 　(5)Australian （澳洲） 2. 種類 Chardonnay（法） 　(1)Chenin Blanc（法） 　(2)Merlot（義、瑞） 　(3)Pinot Noir（法、瑞） 　(4)Zinfandel（美國加州）
aperitif	【法】開胃酒（為增加食慾在餐前所飲的白葡萄酒等）

服務生提問

1. Would you like to start with a cocktail?

　您想以雞尾酒做為餐前酒嗎？

2. Can I get you something to drink?

　要不要喝點什麼？

3. Would you like to start with something to drink?

　首先要不要先喝點東西？

4. What kind/sort/brand?

　哪一種（品牌）的？

5. How would you like your whiskey?

　您的威士忌要怎麼喝？

客人回答

1. Soft / Hard drink

   不含酒精的飲料 / 含酒精的飲料

2. Distilled

   蒸餾（的）

3. On the ice/rock

   加冰塊

4. Neat

   純的；不加冰

5. With soda water/plain water

   加蘇打 / 白開 水

情境會話

(*A guest is ordering a drink*.)

Waiter: What would you like to order?

Guest: I want a double **shot** of whiskey.

Waiter: What brand of whiskey would you **prefer**?

Guest: The Famous Grouse.

Waiter: How would you like it?

Guest: With two **ice cubes**

Waiter: I'll be right back, sir.

（客人正在點飲料）

服務生：您想要點什麼？

客人：我想要兩小杯威士忌。

服務生：您偏好哪個品牌的？

客人：威雀蘇格蘭威士忌。

服務生：您要怎麼喝？

客人：加兩塊冰塊。

服務生：我馬上就好，先生。

1. shot [ʃat] n.（烈酒等的）一口；一小杯
2. prefer [prɪ`fɝ] v. 更喜歡
3. ice cube [aɪs kjub] n. phr. 冰塊

Multiple Choice 單一選擇題

1. Sarah is the _____ in the restaurant.

   (A) order (B) waitress (C) waiter (D) operator

2. A: Excuse me, sir. How many are in your _____?

    B: Four.

   (A) party (B) area (C) smoking (D) reservation

3. I'm extremely sorry, sir. Our restaurant is_____ now. Would
   you please wait for about ten minutes?

   (A) vacant (B) available (C) shared (D) full

4. I am Jason Wang. I have a reservation _____.

   (A) right this place (B) under my name (C) on the list

   (D) in the hotel

5. Sir, may I take your _____ now?

   (A) smoke (B) seat (C) party (D) order

6. I'll be back _____. （選錯誤的）

   (A) soon

   (B) right away

   (C) this way

   (D) immediately

7. Would you like to sit in smoking or _____ area?

   (A) unsmoking (B) no smoke (C) non-smoking (D) not smoking

8. I'm sorry, sir. The non-smoking section is full.

     _____

    (A) May I take your order now?

    (B) Do you have reservation?

    (C) How is your steak?

    (D) Would you like to sit in the smoking section?

9. I'm sorry, ma'am. The tables are _____ tonight.

    (A) right back (B) available (C) fully booked (D) totally free

10. I'm sorry. All of our tables are full at the _____. But there will be tables after 6:30.

    (A) moment (B) book (C) table (D) minute

11. We will have a table for you in _____ twenty minutes.

    (A) within (B) less than (C) right now (D) rather than

12. A: How many people are in your party?

    B: _____

    A: Please come this way.

    (A) Order.

    (B) Twice.

    (C) Smoking.

    (D) Five.

13. A: _____

    B: No, ma'am, I'm sorry. That area is full at the moment.

    (A) How long would we have to wait?

(B) Do you have seats in the non-smoking area?

(C) Do you have free time?

(D) Can you give me a towel?

14. A: Here is your seat.

B: Thank you.

A: Here is the menu. _____

B: OK.

(A) I'll be right back to take your order.

(B) Is everything OK?

(C) How was your meal?

(D) Do you mind sharing a table with others?

15. Host: _____ Your waiter will be here shortly.

Have a nice dinner.

John: Thank you.

(A) Our tables is fully booked tonight.

(B) How many are in your party?

(C) Here is your table, Mr. Jackson.

(D) Do you have a reservation?

16. Host: Good evening. _____

Customer: Six.

Host: I'm sorry, sir. We have no table for six right now. But we

have a table for four.

(A) Party of five?

(B) Would you like a window seat?

(C) Follow me, please.

(D) How would you like your whiskey?

17. Host: _____

Candy: Yes. It's fine.

Host: Your waiter will be right with you.

Candy: Thank you.

(A) How many are in your party?

(B) Do you have a reservation?

(C) Is this table OK?

(D) Would you like something to drink?

18. Candy: We won't have to wait for long, will we?

Hostess: No, ma'am. There should be a table in less than fifteen

minutes. _____

Candy: Thank you.

(A) Would you like to wait?

(B) I'll notify you when your table is ready.

(C) Please come again another time

(D) At least half an hour.

19. Host: Good evening.

Candy: How long would we have to wait? We'd like to sit in the

non-smoking section.

Host: _____

Candy: That's fine. We'd wait.

(A) At least four days.

(B) Less than ten minutes.

(C) Three time a day.

(D) Within a week.

20. Candy: We have a reservation under my name.

Host: _____

Candy: Candy.

Host: Yes, Miss Candy. Come this way, please.

(A) Do you have a reservation?

(B) How long can you wait?

(C) May I have your name, please?

(D) Your waiter will be here in a minute to take your order.

答案： (B)(A)(D)(B)(D)(C)(C)(D)(C)(A)

(B)(D)(B)(A)(B)(A)(C)(B)(B)(C)

Ordering and Serving the Food

7 餐廳點菜與上菜

 本章摘要

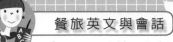

Introduction 學習重點

　　本章進入餐廳服務的核心。一個侍者能否精準的介紹餐廳的餐點，最能看出一個侍者的專業素養的部分，不論是材料、作法、佐料及其他相關細節，都必須相當熟悉。此外，從送茶水及上菜的細節，也可以看出一個侍者對工作的熱忱以及是否受過專業訓練。

Useful Words 常用字彙

肉類

beef	牛肉
chicken	雞肉
mutton	羊肉
pork	豬肉
veal	小牛肉

海鮮

crab	蟹
fish	魚
lobster	龍蝦
oyster	蠔
shrimp	蝦

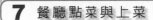
常見的菜單

Apple Pie (a la mode)	蘋果派
Baked Salmon with White Wine	白酒烤鮭魚
Banana Split	香蕉船
Broiled Baby Back Ribs	碳烤乳豬肋排
Buffalo Hot Wings	水牛城辣雞翅
Caesar Salad	凱撒沙拉
Cheesecake	乳酪蛋糕
Chef Salad	主廚沙拉
Clam Chowder	蛤蜊濃湯
Creamy Corn Soup	玉米濃湯
Deep-Fried Onion Rings	酥炸洋蔥圈
Espresso	義大利濃縮咖啡
Fried Calamari	炸花枝圈
Green Salad	生菜沙拉
Grilled French Rack of Lamb	烤小羊排
House Salad	招牌沙拉
Lasagna	千層麵
Lemonade	檸檬汁
Mozzarella Sticks	馬芝瑞拉起士條
New York Strip Steak	紐約牛排
Onion Soup	洋蔥湯
Roast Chicken	烤雞
Shrimp Cocktail	鮮蝦沙拉
Sirloin Steak	沙朗牛排
Sundae	聖代

雞蛋的煮法

eggs Benedict	班尼迪克蛋（英式鬆餅配上水煮蛋、火腿、培根及荷蘭醬）
hard-boiled egg	煮得全熟的蛋
omelet	煎蛋餅
poached egg	水煮荷包蛋
scrambled egg	炒蛋
soft-boiled egg	半熟的水煮蛋
sunny-side up	太陽蛋，即單煎一面的荷包蛋
fried eggs over-easy/hard	煎蛋（嫩煎的／全煎熟的）

Serving a Menu 送菜單

Useful Expressions 常用的表達方法

問候與自我介紹

1. Good evening, my name is＿＿＿ . Please let me know if there's anything you need.

   晚安，我的名字是 ＿＿＿＿＿＿ 。如果您有任何需要，請讓我知道。

2. Hi, my name's ＿＿＿＿＿＿ . I'll be your waiter/server this evening.

   嗨，我的名字是 ＿＿＿＿＿＿ 。我將是您今晚的服務生。

3. Hello, how are you this evening?

   哈囉，今晚好嗎？

4. Is there anything you need me to explain?

有沒有需要我為您解釋的？

給客人看菜單，稍後回來

1. Here are your menus. Let me know when you're ready to order.

這是您的菜單。當您準備好要點餐時，請讓我知道。

2. I'll be with you in few minutes.

我將在幾分鐘之後回來。

3. I'll come back to take your orders in a few minutes.

我將在幾分鐘之後回來為您點餐。

Conversation 會話

(*A waitress is **serving** a menu.*)

Waitress: Good evening. How are you today?

Kyle & Jennifer: Fine, thank you.

Waitress: I'll be your Waitress this evening. My name is Betty. Here's your menu.

Kyle & Jennifer: Thank you.

Waitress: Would you like something to drink while you're looking at your menu?

Kyle: Yes, I'll have a coke, please.

Jennifer: And I'll have a black tea, please.

Waitress: A coke and a black tea. Ok, I'll be right back with your drinks.

（女服務生正在送菜單。）

女服務生：晚安。你們今天好嗎？

凱爾和珍妮佛：很好，謝謝你。

女服務生：我將是你們今晚的服務生。我叫貝蒂。這是你們的菜單。

凱爾和珍妮佛：謝謝你。

女服務生：當你們在看菜單的時候，要不要喝個東西呢？

凱爾：好的，請給我可樂。

珍妮佛：好的，請給我紅茶。

女服務生：一杯可樂及一杯紅茶。好的，我會馬上為你們送上飲料。

Word Bank 重要單字片語

1. serve [sɜv] v. 供應(+with)；侍候（顧客等）；供應（飯菜）；端上

Explaining Dishes 介紹菜內容

Useful Expressions 常用的表達方法
烹煮方式

bake	在爐中烤
deep fry	油炸
fry	油煎
grill	在架上烤
roast	烤
simmer	溫火慢煮
steam	蒸
stir	攪動
boil	（水等）沸騰；開；滾
poach	水煮（低於100度）；隔水燉
stew	燉

例句：通常用被動式(beV+p.p.)

1. The oysters **are smoked**. 這牡蠣是煙燻的。

2. **Is** the steak **grilled**? 這牛排是火烤的嗎？

烹煮程序

to **fillet** the sardines將沙丁魚去骨切片	將（肉）去骨切片
to **slice** the cucumber把小黃瓜切片	把…切成薄片
to **mash** the taro把芋頭搗成泥	把…搗成糊狀
to **stuff** the green pepper 填塞青辣椒	填塞
to **peel** the corn把玉米剝皮	剝皮
to **marinate** the chicken with spicy sauce 用香料醬汁浸泡雞肉	把…浸泡在滷汁中
to **mix** milk and tea 混合牛奶和茶	混合
to **chop** the pork 剁碎豬肉	剁碎
to **mince** the beef 絞碎牛肉	絞碎
to **grate** the carrot 把胡蘿蔔刨絲	刨絲
to **dice/cube** the ham 把火腿切丁	切丁
to **beat** the egg white 打蛋白	打

調味品

curry	咖哩
ginger	薑
mustard	芥末
soy sauce	醬油
vinegar	醋
salt	鹽

pepper	胡椒
nutmeg	荳蔻
olive oil	橄欖油
garlic	蒜
chili sauce	辣椒醬
chili pepper	辣椒
salad dressing	沙拉醬
sugar	糖
ketchup	番茄醬

口味的描述

salty	鹹的
sweet	甜的
sour	酸的
tangy	味道強烈的
bland	味道淡的
delicious	好吃的
tasteless	沒有味道的
spicy	辣的
bitter	苦的
hot	燙的；辣的
fresh	新鮮的
tender	嫩的
juicy	多汁的
crispy	酥脆的
thick/thin	濃／稀

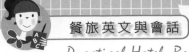
Conversation 會話

(*A waitress is explaining the dishes.*)

Waitress: Would you like to order now?

Guest: Could you recommend something that doesn't take too long to **prepare**? I'm in a hurry.

Waitress: Our pasta special doesn't take very long.

Guest: What is it?

Waitress: Fettuccini Alfredo served with garlic bread and a garden salad.

Guest: Hm, sounds good. I'll have that.

Waitress: And what kind of **dressing** would you like on your salad? We have Italian, French, and Blue Cheese.

Guest: I'll have Italian.

Waitress: OK. So, that's a Fettuccini Alfredo pasta special and a salad with Italian dressing. I'll make sure the chef knows you're in a hurry.

Guest: Thank you. I really appreciate that.

（女服務生正在介紹餐點。）

女服務生：您現在可以點餐了嗎？

客人：你可以推薦不用花太久時間準備的餐點嗎？我有點趕時間。

女服務生：我們的義大利麵特餐不用花太久。

客人：那是什麼？

女服務生：羅馬式奶油白醬麵，包含香蒜麵包以及田園沙拉。

客人：聽起來不錯。那我就點這個吧。

女服務生：那你沙拉上的淋醬要用那一種？我們有義式、法式，還有藍起司。

客人：那我要義式的。

女服務生：好的，一份羅馬式奶油白醬麵特餐，還有義式醬汁的沙拉。我一定會讓廚師知道您在趕時間。

客人：謝謝你。我真的很感激。

Word Bank 重要單字片語

1. prepare [prɪˋpɛr] v. 準備；做（飯菜）；製作；調製

2. dressing [ˋdrɛsɪŋ] n.（拌沙拉等用的）調料

大哉問：請問dressing與sauce有什麼不同？		
sauce	食物（通常是主餐或甜點）上的醬汁（用淋的或沾的）	What kind of sauce would you like on your ice cream? sauce (1) mustard sauce（芥末醬）(2) white wine sauce（白酒醬汁）
dressing	淋在沙拉上的醬汁	Would you like Italian or French dressing?
		salad dressing沙拉醬：(1) Thousand Island（千島）(2) Italian Dressing（義式）(3) French Dressing（法式）

Quiz I 小試身手：請寫出正確英文單字

Part I

1. The vegetables are s_____. 蔬菜是用蒸的。

2. The potatoes are b_____. 馬鈴薯是在爐中烤的。

3. The salmon is g_____. 鮭魚是用火在架上烤的

答案：1. steamed 2. baked 3. grilled

Part II：請填入適當的形容詞，每格填入一個最適當的字。

> sour fresh tender crispy spicy juicy sweet

1. Vinegar is _____.

2. The apple pie is _____.

3. This oyster is _____.

4. The watermelon is _____.

5. The fried chicken is _____.

6. Chili sauce is_____.

7. The steak is _____.

答案：1. sour 2. sweet 3. fresh 4. juicy 5. crispy 6. spicy 7. tender

Part III：請把動詞搭配合適的名詞

Verbs	Nouns
1. peel	a. the water
2. bake	b. the butter and sugar
3. boil	c. the potato
4. mince	d. the beef
5. mix	e. the cookies

答案：1. c 2. e 3. a 4. f 5. b

Taking the Order 點餐

Useful Expressions 常用的表達方法

詢問客人是否準備好

1. Are you ready to order?

   您準備好要點餐了嗎？

2. May I take your order?

   我可以幫您點餐了嗎？

3. Would you like to order now?

   您現在要點餐了嗎？

客人還未準備好

1. We are not ready to order yet.

   我們還沒準備好點餐。

2. I haven't decided yet.

   我還沒決定。

3. Could you give us a few more minutes?

   可以再多給我幾分鐘嗎？

4. We need a few more minutes to decide.

   我們需要多幾分鐘來決定。

點餐時客人可能會問

1. What's the soup of the day?

   今日特湯是什麼？

2. What's the special of the day?

   今日特餐是什麼？

3. What do you recommend?

你推薦什麼？

4. Does the steak come with a salad?

牛排有附沙拉嗎？

5. What's in this dish?

餐點裡面有什麼？

點餐時詢問客人

1. How would you like your steak?

您的牛排要幾分熟？

2. What kind of potatoes would you like? Mashed, baked, or French fries?

您想要怎樣的馬鈴薯？是薯泥、洋芋、還是炸薯條呢？

3. Would you like soup or salad with that?

您想要附湯或沙拉嗎？

4. What kind of dressing would you like for your salad?

您的沙拉想要什麼淋醬？

5. What would you like to drink?

您想要喝什麼？

6. Would you like to order some wine to go with that?

您想要點酒來搭配嗎？

	What's...? What's this dish here? Can you tell me about this?
客人：這是道什麼菜？	
服務生： 它是一種 _____。 這道菜是由_____和_____做成的。 這道菜裡面有放_____和_____。	It's a sort of _____. It consists of _____ and _____. It's made from _____. It contains _____.

例句：

1. Guest: Can you tell me about your minestrone soup? (vegetables, beans, pasta)

    Waiter: It contains vegetables, beans, and pasta.

    客人：你可以介紹一下義大利濃湯嗎？

    服務生：有蔬菜、豆子及義大利空心麵。

2. Guest: What's in your salad?

    Waiter: It's made from lettuce and smoked chicken breast.

    客人：沙拉裡面有什麼？

    服務生：是用萵苣及煙燻雞胸肉做成的。

客人：這道菜有附白飯嗎？ 　　　這道菜有附任何東西嗎？	Does it come with rice? What's it served with? What does it come with? Is there anything to go with it?
服務生：有，這道菜有附…。 　　　　沒有，這道菜沒有任何附餐。	Yes, it comes with _____. Yes, it's served with _____. No, it's served on its own.

例句：

Guest: What is in your house salad?(lettuce, cucumber, tomatoes, Italian dressing)

Waiter: It **consists of** lettuce, tomatoes, and cucumber, and **it's served with** Italian dressing.

客人：招牌沙拉裡有什麼？

服務生：包括萵苣、番茄、小黃瓜，配上義大利式的醬汁。

Conversation 1 會話一

（*The waiter is going to take the order, but the guests are not ready*.）

Waiter: May I take your order now?

Guest: Could you give me a few more minutes?

Waiter: Sure, please **take your time**. I'll come back when you are ready.

（服務生正想要客人點餐，但客人還沒準備好）

服務生：現在可以幫您點餐了嗎？

客人：你可以多給我幾分鐘嗎？

服務生：當然，請慢慢來。當您準備好了，我再回來。

Word Bank 重要單字片語

1. Take your time. 慢慢來

Conversation 2 會話二

(*The guests are ready to order, and the waiter patiently takes the order*.)

Waiter: What would you like to order?

Guest: Hm..., I think I will have a "New York Steak".

Waiter: How would you like your steak...**rare**, **medium**, or **well done**?

Guest: Hm..., medium rare.

Waiter: Very well, and how would you like your eggs?

Guest: **Poached**.

Waiter: And would you like your poached eggs with bacon, sausages, or ham?

Guest: Sausage, please.

Waiter: What would you like to drink?

Guest: Um..., coffee and orange juice please.

Waiter: Will there be anything else?

Guest: No, that's all.

Waiter: Just a few minutes, please.

（客人準備好要點餐，服務生有耐心的為他們點餐。）

服務生：您想要點什麼？

客人：我想我要一份紐約牛排。

服務生：您想要牛排幾分熟？二分、五分，還是全熟？

客人：三分熟。

服務生：很好，那您的蛋的？

客人：水煮的荷包蛋。

服務生：那您的蛋要搭配培根、臘腸、還是火腿呢？

客人：臘腸，謝謝。

服務生：您想要喝什麼？

客人：請給我咖啡和柳橙汁。

服務生：還有其他東西嗎？

客人：沒有了。

服務生：請稍待片刻。

Word Bank 重要單字片語

1. rare [rɛr] adj. 生的

2. medium [`midɪəm] adj. 五分熟；半熟

3. well done [wɛl dʌn] adj. 全熟

4. poached [potʃd] adj. 水煮的

大哉問：關於牛排要幾分熟的說法。	
rare	一～二分熟
medium rare	三分熟
medium	五分熟
medium well	七分熟
well done	全熟

Conversation 3 會話三

（*The waiter is taking the order for breakfast.*）

Waiter: Are you ready to order?

Guest: Yes, I would like this one.

Waiter: **American-Style Breakfast**. What kind of juice would you like?

Guest: Orange juice, please.

Waiter: How would you like your eggs?

Guest: Scrambled.

Waiter: Would you like ham or bacon with that?

Guest: I would like the ham.

Waiter: Sure, sir. Would you like toast or a roll?

Guest: A roll, please.

Waiter: Would you like coffee or tea?

Guest: Coffee.

Waiter: The American-Style Breakfast set-, so that's orange juice, scrambled eggs with ham, a roll and coffee. Is that right?

Guest: Yes, that's right.

Waiter: Thank you. I'll be right back with your coffee.

（服務生正在為客人點早餐。）

服務生：您準備好要點餐了嗎？

客人：是的，我想要這個。

服務生：美式早餐一份。請問您要喝什麼果汁？

客人：柳橙汁，謝謝。

服務生：您想要蛋怎麼烹煮？

客人：炒蛋。

服務生：您想要搭配火腿還是培根？

客人：我想要火腿。

服務生：當然。您想要吐司還是捲餅？

客人：捲餅。

服務生：您想要喝茶還是咖啡？

客人：咖啡。

服務生：美式早餐一份，有柳橙汁、火腿炒蛋、捲餅以及咖啡。對
　　　　嗎？

客人：沒錯。

服務生：謝謝您。咖啡馬上來。

Word Bank 重要單字片語

1. American-style breakfast n. phr. 美式早餐

大哉問：請問歐陸早餐(Continental Breakfast)與美式早餐 (American Breakfast)有什麼不同？
歐陸早餐(Continental Breakfast) 不包含蛋或肉類，比較清淡、份量較少，以咖啡麵包為主
美式早餐(American Breakfast) Brunch 美式早午餐 份量較重，通常有一肉類主餐，如牛排、火腿、培根或肉腸，外加鬆餅、薯餅、蛋、咖啡及柳橙汁等。與歐式早餐最大的差別就是有熱食。
英式早餐(British Breakfast) 果汁、奶油烤吐司、兩個蛋、煎培根、煎火腿、煎香腸、布丁、炒蘑菇、烤蕃茄、馬鈴薯餅、煮豆子，另外搭配英式早餐茶，如熱奶茶等。

Quiz I 小試身手

Part I：請根據提示，試著回答客人的問題

Guest: What's in your breakfast? (orange juice, whole wheat bread, waffles, and scrambled egg.)

Waiter:_____.

客人：早餐有什麼？

服務生：包含柳橙汁、全麥麵包、鬆餅、及炒蛋。

答案：It contains/consists of orange juice, whole wheat bread, waffles, and scrambled egg.

Part I：請填入適當的字詞

Dialog A

Waiter: Would you like to_____ from the menu?

Guest: Yes, please.

Waiter: Here is our breakfast _____.

Guest: Thank you very much.

Waiter: What_____ you like?

Guest: I'd like cornflakes and two pieces of toast _____ butter, please.

答案：order, menu, would, with

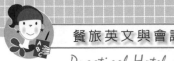
Dialog B

Waiter: Would you like to order now, ma'am.?

Guest: What would you_____?

Waiter: Today's _____ is very good... _____ chicken with

　　　　spinach and _____ potatoes.

Guest: That sounds good. I'll take today's special.

Waiter: Would you like a salad, madam?

Guest: A tomato salad, please.

Waiter: And to drink?

Guest: A small _____ of rose.

Waiter: Very good, madam.

答案：recommend/suggest, special, grilled, baked, bottle

Dialog C

Waiter: Would you like to start with an_____?

Guest: Yes, I'd like a shrimp cocktail.

Waiter: Would you like_____?

Guest: Clam chowder, please.

Waiter: And to _____?

Guest: A bottle of Heineken.

Waiter: Is that all for you, Ms.?

Guest: I want to see your menu.

Waiter: Right _____.

答案：appetizer, soup, drink, away

Offering a Drink 送茶水

Useful Expressions 常用的表達方法

在客人看菜單時，可先提供飲料，讓他們可以一邊喝一邊考慮。

1. Would you like to order something to drink first?

   您要先點東西喝嗎？

2. Would you like to order something to drink while you are looking at the menu?

   當您在看菜單的時候要先點東西喝嗎？

3. Would you like to start with something to drink?

   您一開始要先喝點什麼嗎？

4. Can I get you something to drink?

   我可以為您準備什麼喝的嗎？

Conversation 會話

(*A waiter is asking to serve a drink*)

Waiter: Is this table all right with you?

Guest: Yes, that's fine.

Waiter: Here is the menu. Can I get you something to drink?

Guest: Yes, I would like **red wine**, please.

Waiter: Would you like your red wine with ice?

Guest: Yes, with one **cube** of ice.

Waiter: I will be right back with your drink.

（服務生正在詢問是否要上茶水。）

服務生：座位還滿意嗎？

客人：滿意，謝謝你。

服務生： 這是菜單。我可以為您準備什麼喝的嗎？

客人：是的，請給我紅酒。

服務生： 您的紅酒要加冰嗎？

客人：是的，一塊冰塊。

服務生： 馬上來。

Word Bank 重要單字片語

1. red wine n. phr. 紅酒

2. cube [kjub] n. 立方體（在此指冰塊）

Quiz 小試身手：請寫出正確英文單字

1. Would you like to o_____ something to d_____ while you are
   looking at the menu?
   當您在看菜單的時候要先點東西喝嗎？

2. Can I g_____ you s_____ to drink?
   我可以為您準備什麼喝的嗎？

答案：order, drink, get, something

Serving the Meal 上菜

Useful Expressions 常用的表達方法

菜單的各個部分

	也被稱為…	可能包括哪些…
Appetizers 開胃菜	Appies, Finger Food, Combo Platters, Snacks, Starters	Garlic Bread（香蒜麵包）, Cheese Plate（起司盤）, Nachos（墨西哥玉米餅）
Salads (and Soups) 沙拉和湯	Garden Fresh, Greens, Light Fare, Lighter Favorites, Low Calorie Choices, Low-fat Selections	Caesar Salad（凱薩沙拉）, Soup of the Day（每日一湯）
Sandwiches 三明治	Burgers, From the Deli, From the Grill, Lunch Menu, Wraps	Grilled Chicken Sandwich（烤雞三明治）, Veggie (Garden) Burger（蔬菜田園漢堡）, Steak Sandwich（牛排三明治）
Italian 義大利式的餐點	Noodles, Pasta, Pizza	Spaghetti（義大利麵）, Pepperoni Pizza（臘腸披薩）
Main Course 主餐	Entrée, Dinners, Main Dish, Main Event	New York Steak（紐約牛排）, Pork Chops（豬排）
Sides 配菜	Accompaniments, On the Side, Side Dishes	French Fries（薯條）, Rice（飯）, Grilled Veggies（烤蔬菜）

Seafood 海鮮	Catch of the day, Fish, Fresh from the Sea	Fish and Chips（炸魚及薯條），Smoked Salmon（煙燻鮭魚）
Mexican 墨西哥式的口味：德州墨西哥式的	South of the Border, Tex-Mex	Fajitas（法士達），Nachos（臘腸），Enchiladas（以玉米餅包裹牛肉或雞肉，佐以醬料或起司烘烤。）
Specialties 特餐	Signature items, Favorites, Pleasers, 5 Stars	BBQ Ribs（烤肋排），Hot Wings（哈辣雞翅），Chicken Cordon Bleu（藍帶豬排）
Desserts 點心	Sweets, Treats, For the Sweet Tooth	Apple Pi（蘋果派），Mocha Cheesecake（摩卡芝士蛋糕），Banana Split（香蕉船）
Beverages 飲料	Drinks, Non-alcoholic beverages, Refreshments	Soda Pop（汽水），Juice（果汁），Milk（牛奶）
Wine and Beer 酒類	Coolers, Draft, Liquor, Specialty Drinks, Spirits, From the Bar	Brandy（白蘭地）、Champagne（香檳）、GIN（琴酒）、Long Island Iced Tea（長島冰茶）
Kids Menu 兒童特餐	Juniors, Kids Stuff, Little Tikes, For the Munchkins	Spaghetti and Meatballs（肉丸子義大利麵），Cheeseburger（起司漢堡），Chicken Fingers（雞柳條）

Conversation 會話

(*A waiter is serving pork chops*.)

Waiter: Here is your order of pork chops. The plate is hot. Please be careful.

Guest: Thank you. I'll **watch out for** it! It looks delicious.

Waiter: You're welcome. Enjoy your meal. If there is anything I can do to help, please let me know.

（服務生正在上豬排。）

服務生：這是您的餐點。豬排。盤子很燙，請小心。

客人：謝謝你。我會注意的。看起來很好吃。

服務生：不客氣。祝您用餐愉快。如果有我可以幫忙的地方，請讓我知道。

Word Bank 重要單字片語

1. watch out for v. phr. 小心提防；注意

Quiz 小試身手：配合題

Part I

1.	Dessert	a	Chef Brian's home-style chili
2.	Starters	b	Homemade Iced Tea
3.	Specialties	c	Lemon and herb glazed Salmon
4.	Refreshments	d	tiramisu
5.	Seafood	e	Mouth watering garlic cheese toast

答案: 1d, 2e, 3a, 4b, 5c

Part II

1.	Sides	f	Loaded mashed potatoes
2.	Kids Menu	g	Big Daddy's Hamburger with fresh cut fries Chef Brian's home-style chili
3.	Sandwiches	h	Junior Spaghetti and Meatballs
4.	Spirits	i	Seasonal tossed greens
5.	Salads	j	1/2 liter house white

答案: 6f, 7h, 8g, 9j, 10i

Extension 延伸學習：接受客房服務訂餐

接到電話時的問候

1. Good morning/afternoon/evening, room service.

   早安 / 午安 / 晚安，客房服務。

2. Room service. May I help you?

   客房服務。有需要幫忙的地方嗎？

回答客人可能的問題

1. Breakfast is available from 6:00 a.m. to 10:30 a.m.

   早餐在早上六點到十點半供應。

2. You'll find the menu for room service in the stationery folder in your room.

   你將可以在房間的文件夾找到客房服務的菜單。

詢問房號

1. May I have your room number, please?

   請問你的房號？

關於上菜的時間

1. At what time shall we serve it?

   我們方便什麼時候上菜？

2. I'll have your breakfast sent up to you as soon as possible, sir.

   先生，我會盡快將您的早餐送上來。

3. It should take about twenty minutes, sir.

   先生，大約要花二十分鐘。

4. Your order should be there in about fifteen minutes.

您的餐點將在大約十五分鐘後送來。

情境會話

(*A hotel guest is calling for room service*.)

Room Service: Room Service. May I help you?

Guest: Yes. I would like to order lunch.

Room Service: Certainly, sir. May I take your order, please?

Guest: Yes, I'd like beef curry rice, a salad and some beer.

Room Service: Certainly, sir. Which brand of beer do you prefer?

Guest: Taiwan beer.

Room Service: How many bottles would you like?

Guest: Two, please.

Room Service: How many glasses will you need?

Guest: Just one.

Room Service: I see. Will that be all?

Guest: Yes.

Room Service: Thank you, sir. Your order should be ready in about twenty minutes.

Guest: Fine. Thank you.

（飯店的客人打電話要求客房服務。）

客房服務：客房服務，有需要幫忙的地方嗎？

客人：是的，我想點午餐。

客房服務：好的，先生。現在可以點餐了嗎？

客人：是的，我要咖哩牛肉飯、沙拉、以及啤酒。

客房服務：好的，先生。你想要哪一個品牌的啤酒呢？

客人：台灣啤酒。

客房服務: 你想要幾罐呢？

客人：兩罐，謝謝。

客房服務: 你需要幾個杯子呢？

客人：只要一個。

客房服務: 我懂了。這就是全部了嗎？

客人：是的。

客房服務：謝謝您，先生。您的餐點將在大約二十分鐘後送達。

客人：很好，謝謝你。

Multiple Choice 單一選擇題

1. I _____ our Fajitas. It is very delicious.

   (A) reserve (B) recommend (C) name (D) notify

2. That soup is too _____. I want to drink some water.

   (A) delicious (B) fresh (C) juicy (D) spicy

3. A: What's your _____ today?

    B: Baked salmon with white wine.

   (A) salad (B) desert (C) special (D)soup of the day

4. I will have a _____ of creamy corn soup.

   (A) roll (B) bowl (C) breast (D) glass

5. I would like a small _____ tea.

   (A) mustard (B) poached (C) iced (D) sliced

6. What type of _____ would you like on your salad? French or Italian?

   (A) sauce (B) flavor (C) drinking (D) dressing

7. _____ is an Italian food.

   (A) Stingy tofu (B) Cheese cake (C) Grilled chicken sandwich
   (D) Spaghetti

8. Fajitas is a/an _____ food.

   (A) Italian (B) American (C) Mexican (D) French

9. Juice and tea are _____. (選錯的)

   (A) beverages (B) soft drinks (C) salad dressings

   (D) refreshments

10. My friend likes to eat _____ chicken and drink Coke in the fast

    food restaurant.

   (A) mashed (B) fried (C) iced (D) marinated

11. Waiter: Here are your menus. _____

    Jim: OK. Thank you.

   (A) How would you like your steak?

   (B) Would you like to order some wine to go with that?

   (C) I'll be back in a minute to take your order.

   (D) Would you like to take your order now?

12. Jack: _____

    Waiter: New York steak.

   (A) What's your special today?

   (B) What's your name?

   (C) What's in this dish?

   (D) What's the soup of today?

13. Cindy: _____

    Waiter: How about the grilled salmon?

    Cindy: OK.

   (A) Do you have the reservation?

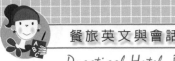
(B) What do you recommend today?

(C) I'm ready to order.

(D) What's it in the soup?

14. Waitress: Are you ready to order?

Mary: _____ I'd like pork chops.

Waitress: Sure, I'll be right back, ma'am.

(A) Yes, I think so.

(B) The soup is cold.

(C) Does it come with anything?

(D) No, we need more time.

15. Waiter: Here is your order, sir. Pork chops.

Guest: Thank you.

Waiter: You're welcome. Enjoy your meal. _____

(A) I'll have the grilled chicken sandwich.

(B) It is served with the soup of the day.

(C) If there is anything I can help, please let me know.

(D) I'll be your waiter tonight.

16. Waiter: _____

Kyle: Thousand Island.

Waiter: OK. Thank you, sir.

(A) Would you like to have a cup of coffee?

(B) Is everything satisfactory?

(C) How was your meal?

(D) What kind of dressing would you like on your salad?

17. Waiter: Are you ready to order?

    Ken: Yes. I'll have the grilled chicken.

    Waiter: _____

    Ken: I will have French fries.

    (A) What side dish would you like?

    (B) Would you like something to drink?

    (C) I'll come back in a moment.

    (D) How about a glass of red wine?

18. Waiter: What would you like to order?

    Guest: I think I will have a "New York Steak".

    Waiter:_____

    Guest: Well done.

    (A) How would you like your whiskey?

    (B) How would you like your steak?

    (C) Would you like a black tea with sugar?

    (D) It comes with a salad.

19. Waiter: What would you like to drink?

    Gary: Coffee and orange juice, please.

    Waiter: _____

    Gary: No, that's all.

    (A) Is the food OK?

    (B) Are you satisfied with the meal?

(C) Is there anything else?

(D) Are you ready to order?

20. Guest: Is the steak grilled?

Waitress: _____.

(A) Yes, it's fried.

(B) No, it's grilled.

(C) Yes, it isn't.

(D) No, it's fried.

答案： (C)(D)(C)(B)(C)(D)(D)(C)(C)(B)

(C)(A)(B)(A)(C)(D)(A)(B)(C)(D)

Service During the Meal

8 用餐中的服務

 本章摘要

Taking Plates 換碗盤

Cleaning the Table 清理桌面

Refilling Drinks 補充水酒

Extension 延伸學習

Introduction 學習重點

讓客人有一個美好的用餐經驗，一個侍者的服務態度與專業度是非常重要的。在用餐當中，換煙灰缸、換碗盤、清理桌面、補充水酒等等服務，每一個細節都相當重要，在本章中我們將來看看這些情境對話。

Useful Words 常用字彙

water glass	水杯
cup	咖啡杯
saucer	杯碟
spoon	湯匙
dinner knife	餐刀
steak knife	牛排刀
place mat	餐具墊
bread plate	麵包碟
plate	盤子
butter knife	奶油刀
napkin	餐巾
wineglass	酒杯
dinner fork	餐叉
salad fork	沙拉叉
butter	奶油
table cloth	桌布 / 檯布
salt and pepper shakers	胡椒、鹽粉末罐

Taking Plates 換碗盤

Useful Expressions 常用的表達方法

1. How is everything?

   一切還好嗎？

2. How was the food today?

   今天的食物怎樣？

3. How was your meal?

   您的餐點怎麼樣？

4. Is everything OK?

   一切還好嗎？

5. Are you enjoying your meal?

   用餐愉快嗎？

6. Did you enjoy your meal?

   您喜歡您的餐點嗎？

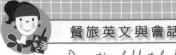
Conversation 會話

(*A waiter is asking if he can take the plate away.*）

Waiter: How was your meal?

Guest: The food was delicious.

Waiter: Are you **finished**? May I take your plate?

Guest: Yes.

(*The waiter takes out the plates and* **replaces** *them with clean ones.*）

Waiter: Enjoy your meal.

（服務生正在詢問是否可以收走盤子。）

服務生：您的餐點怎麼樣？

客人：食物很好吃。

服務生：您吃完了嗎？我可以收您的盤子了嗎？

客人：可以。

（服務生把盤子收走，且用乾淨的盤子取代。）

服務生：祝您用餐愉快。

Word Bank 重要單字片語

1. finish [ˋfɪnɪʃ] v. 用完；吃完

2. replace [rɪˋples] v. 取代；以…代替

Quiz 小試身手：請寫出正確英文單字

Waiter: Is there anything I can help, sir?

Guest: Could you please t_____ a_____ this ashtray（煙灰
缸）and give me a_____ one?

Waiter: Certainly, sir. I'll bring a c_____ one l_____.

答案：take, away, another, clear, later

Cleaning the Table 清理桌面

Useful Expressions 常用的表達方法

服務生詢問顧客是否用餐完畢（可以收盤子）

1. Are you finished or still working on it?

   請問您已經用完了還是還在吃呢？

2. Excuse me. Are you finished? May I take your plate?

   對不起，您用完了嗎？我可幫您收盤子嗎？

顧客的回答

1. I'm finished. 我已經用餐完畢了。

2. I'm still working on it. 我還在用。

Conversation 會話

（*A waiter is about to clear the table*.）

Waiter: Excuse me. Are you finished with that?

Guest: Yes, thanks.

Waiter: I'll **get** these **out of your way**. How was your meal?

Guest: Delicious, thank you.

Waiter: Would you like some coffee or tea?

Guest: Tea would be great.

Waiter: Sure. Would you like sugar with that?

Guest: No, thanks.

Waiter: Was everything all right with your meals?

Guest: Yes, we like them very much, and your **service** is good.

Waiter: Thank you. It's my pleasure to hear that.

（服務生正準備清理桌面。）

服務生：不好意思。請問您吃完了嗎？

客人：是的，謝謝。

服務生：我會把這些收走。您的餐點還可以嗎？

客人：很好吃，謝謝你。

服務生：您想要喝點咖啡或茶嗎？

客人：茶好了。

服務生：好的，您要加糖嗎？

客人：不用，謝謝。

服務生：您的餐點一切都還好嗎？

客人：是的，我很喜歡，而且你的服務很好。

服務生：謝謝您。我很高興聽到您這麼說。

Word Bank 重要單字片語

1. get sth. out of one's way 把某物移開某人的視線範圍

2. service [ˋsɝs] n. 服務

Quiz 小試身手：請寫出正確英文單字

Waiter: Are you _____ with your salad?

Guest: Yes, I am.

Waiter: I'll _____ that away for you.

Guest: Thank you.

答案：finished, take

Refilling Drinks 補充水酒

Useful Expressions 常用的表達方法

1. Excuse me. Would you like to have some more water?

   對不起，您還需要加水嗎？

2. Would you like to refill the water glass?

   您要加水嗎？

3. Excuse me. Would you care for another bottle of wine?

   對不起，您還要再來一瓶葡萄酒嗎？

4. Would you like some more coffee?

   您要來點咖啡嗎？

Conversation 會話

（*A waiter is offering to refill a guest's drink.*）

Waiter: How was everything?

Guest: Great, thanks.

Waiter: Would you like me to **refill** your wine glass?

Guest: No, thank you. We're OK for now.

Waiter: Good. If there is anything else you need, just let me know.

（服務生正在詢問客人要不要再倒飲料。）

服務生：一切都還好嗎？

客人：很好，謝謝。

服務生：您的酒杯要再加滿酒嗎？

客人：不用了，謝謝。現在這樣就好了。

服務生：好的。如果有其他需要，就讓我知道。

Word Bank 重要單字片語

1. refill [ri`fɪl] v. 再裝滿；再灌滿

Quiz 小試身手：請寫出正確英文單字

1. Would you like to r_____ the water g_____ ?
   您要加水嗎？

2. Would you like some m_____ coffee?
   您要來點咖啡嗎？

答案：refill, glass, more

Extension 延伸學習：客房內餐飲服務並介紹菜

要進房間之前

1. This is room service. May I come in?

   這是客房服務。我可以進來嗎？

詢問餐點 / 餐車 / 托盤該放哪

2. May I place the trolley/tray/cart here?

   我可以把餐車 / 托盤 / 手推車放這嗎？

3. Where should I put the trolley/tray/cart?

   我該把餐車 / 托盤 / 手推車放哪？

4. Where shall I set it?

   我該把餐點放置在哪？

餐車 / 托盤的處置

1. When you are finished, could you leave the tray in the hallway, please?

   當您用餐完畢時，可以請您將托盤放在走廊嗎？

2. We'll send someone to collect your trolley/tray.

   我們將派人來收餐車 / 托盤。

3. You may leave the trolley/tray on the hallway.

   你可以將餐車 / 托盤放在走廊。

詢問可否移動東西

1. May I move these bottles of beer aside?

   我可以把這幾罐啤酒移開嗎？

2. May I put these bottles of beer on the dressing table?

　我可以把這幾罐啤酒放在梳妝台嗎？

情境會話一

(*A waiter is serving the dishes in a room*.)

Waiter: This is Room Service. May I come in?

Guest: Yes, Please.

Waiter: Here is the food you ordered. Where shall I place the tray?

Guest: Please set it over there.

Waiter: Could you sign here, please?

Guest: Sure.

Waiter: Thank you, sir. When you have finished, and wish to have
　　　　your tray removed, please dial number 9 for room service.

Guest: Yes, of course.

Waiter: Thank you, sir. Please enjoy your meal.

（服務生正在房間內上菜。）

服務生：這是客房服務，我可以進來嗎？

客人：是的，請進。

服務生：這是你點的食物。我該把托盤放在哪裡？

客人：請放在這裡。

服務生：可以請你在這簽名嗎？

客人：當然可以。

服務生：謝謝您，先生。當您用餐完畢，想要人來收時，請打分機9找客房服務。

客人：好。

服務生：謝謝您，先生。祝用餐愉快。

情境會話二

(*A waiter is serving the soup in a room*.)

Waiter: May I serve you soup now?

Guest: Yes, please do.

Waiter: There is a **warmer** under the trolley. Please **help yourself** but be careful because it's hot.

Guest: Yes, I will.

Waiter: Thank you, sir.

（服務生正在房間內上湯品。）

服務生：請問我可以上湯了嗎？

客人：好的，請上。

服務生：在餐車下面有一加熱器。請自行取用，但要小心，因為很燙。

客人：好，我會的。

服務生：謝謝您，先生。

1. warmer [ˋwɔrmɚ] n. 加熱器
2. help oneself v. phr. 自行取用

Multiple Choice 單一選擇題

1. _____You don't need to be in a hurry.

   (A) Do you make a reservation? (B) It must be tasty. (C) Make a phone call. (D) Take your time.

2. We don't smoke. There is no need to put the _____ on our table.

   (A) plate (B) ashtray (C) napkin (D) spoon

3. Brandy is a strong _____ drink.

   (A) soft (B) allergic (C) bottle (D) alcoholic

4. I _____ doing my history report.

   (A) order (B) brew (C) finish (D) replace

5. You can use the _____ to protect your clothes when while you are eating in a restaurant.

   (A) napkin (B) ashtray (C) fork (D) table cloth

6. The waiter came here and _____ our glasses.

   (A) refreshed (B) reserved (C) replaced (D) refilled

7. Is everything _____? (選錯的)

   (A) good (B) OK (C) wrong (D) satisfactory

8. Waiter: _____

   David: No, thanks. I'm allergic to alcohol.

   (A) Would you like to refill the water glass?

   (B) It smells good.

(C) How is everything?

(D) Would you like to have some wine?

9. Waiter: May I take your plate away for you?

   Nicole: No. _____

   (A) I have finished my drink.

   (B) Please take me to the restroom.

   (C) I'm ready to order.

   (D) I'm still working on it.

10. Waitress: Would you like a bottle of coke, ma'am?

    Betty: _____ Thank you.

    (A) Anything to drink?

    (B) No, thanks.

    (C) That will be fine.

    (D) I want cappuccino .

11. Waiter: _____

    Jerry: Yes. I'm finished.

    Waiter: Let me take your bowl away.

    (A) Have you finished the steak?

    (B) Are you finished the soup?

    (C) Do you bring your VIP card?

    (D) Are you done with your drink?

12. Ivy: I'm allergic to alcohol. _____

    Waitress: Sure. I'll be right back with the menu.

(A) Do you have red wine?

(B) Do you have any non-alcoholic beverages?

(C) Do you have whiskey?

(D) Do you have an onion soup?

13. Grace: Excuse me, sir.

Waiter: _____

Green: Please bring me a glass of water.

(A) Yes. Can I help you?

(B) Sure. I'll be back right away.

(C) I'm terribly sorry.

(D) May I take your plate away?

14. Bob: Excuse me, sir. I'd like to smoke. _____.

Waiter: Sure, right away, sir.

(A) Please give me a table cloth.

(B) Please bring me a salad fork.

(C) Would you please bring me an ashtray?

(D) Would you please bring me a doggie bag?

15. Elma: Excuse me, waitress.

Waitress: _____

Emma: Please bring me a new knife.

(A) May I have your name, please?

(B) Would you please repeat the message?

(C) Anything else, ma'am?

(D) What can I get for you, miss?

答案：(D)(B)(D)(C)(A)(D)(C)(D)(D)(C)

　　　　(B)(B)(A)(C)(D)

The Cashier and Thanks for Coming

9 出納與送客

 本章摘要

Talking about Money 金額說明

Tax/Service Charge 稅金與服務費說明

Methods of Payment 付款方式

Making Change/Receipts 找零與收據

Exchanging Foreign Currency 換外幣

Check-out 退房付費

Thanks for Coming 道謝與送客

Extension 延伸學習

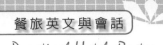
Introduction 學習重點

　　在本章將教你怎麼幫客人結帳。不論是餐廳或是旅館的服務，最後出納與送客，就是要讓客人在享受之後，能夠心滿意足的付錢，所以在帳單金額的計算、費用說明、付款方式、找零錢及開收據，甚至提供換外幣的服務時，都要有耐心並注意禮貌。（註：本章內容將會有本書第一章數詞的應用，同學們可參照第一章，以便複習。）

Useful Words 常用字彙

change	零錢，兌換
pay	付款，支付
service fee	服務費
tip	小費
exchange rate	匯率
foreign currency	外幣
foreign exchange	外匯
cash a check	兌現支票
bill	紙鈔
coin	硬幣

Talking about Money 金額說明

Useful Expressions 常用的表達方法

客人想買單時

1. Could I have my bill, please？

   請問可以幫我結帳嗎？

2. I'd like to settle my bill.

   請幫我結帳。

3. May I have the check, please?

   請問可以幫我結帳嗎？

4. Can you bring us our check, please?

   請幫我們把帳單拿來好嗎？

5. Give me the bill/check, please.

   請給我帳單，謝謝。

6. Where do I pay?

   在哪結帳？

7. Can we have separate bills?

   請問我們能分開結帳嗎？

出納的回應

Your bill comes to_____dollars (plus tax/_____%service charge).

您的帳單一共是_____元（含稅金／百分之_____服務費）。

Conversation 會話

(*A guest is going to check the bill*.)

Guest: Could I have my bill, please？

Cashier: Yes, here you go.

Guest: How much is the bill?

Cashier: It comes to a total of NT$3,250.

Guest: I see. Here you are.

Cashier: Thank you, sir.

(*After a few seconds*...)

Cashier: Thanks for your patience. Here is your change of NT$250.

　　　　Have a nice evening.

（客人正準備付帳。）

客人：請問我可以結帳了嗎？

出納員：好的，這是您的帳單。

客人：多少錢？

出納員：總數是三千兩百二十五元。

客人：好的。給你。

出納員：謝謝您，先生。

（幾秒鐘之後⋯）

出納員：謝謝您的耐心。找您兩百五十元。祝您有個美好的夜晚！

Quiz 小試身手：請寫出正確英文單字

Waiter: Is everything fine w_____ your meal?

Guest: That was excellent.

Waiter: Great, Would you like anything else?

Guest: Yes, I'd like two coffees and the bill.

Waiter: Yes, sir. Do you want one bill or s_____ bills?

Guest: Yes, please. We want separate bills.

Waiter: Right away, sir.

(*After a few seconds*...)

Waiter: That will be NT$1,235.

Guest: H_____ you are.

Waiter: Thanks. Thanks for coming.

答案： with, separate, Here

Tax/Service Charge 稅金與服務費說明

Useful Expressions 常用的表達方法

講解稅金與服務費的算法

1. You don't have to pay any extra for tax. 您不用額外付稅。

2. The tax/service charge had already included in the price of themeal.

   稅金／服務費已經包含在餐點的價錢當中了。

3. Your bill includes a _____% service charge and a _____% tax.

   百分之 _____ 的服務費及百分之 _____ 的稅金已加在您的帳單當中。

4. We add _____ % tax and there is a _____ service charge added to each bill.

   我們加了百分之 _____ 的稅，而每張帳單還附加百分之 _____ 的服務費。

Conversation 會話

（*A cashier is explaining tax and service charge.*）

Guest: May I have the check, please? How much will it be?

Cashier: Thank you, sir. It comes to NT$2,280.

Guest: NT$2,280? I thought it was NT$2,000.

Cashier: Well, 4% tax and 10% service charge are **added** to your bill.

Guest: I see. Do you accept this traveler's check?

Cashier: Yes, we do. Could you please sign here?—Thank you very much. We look forward to serving you again.

（收銀員正在解釋稅金以及服務費。）

客人：請問我可以結帳了嗎？多少錢？

出納員：謝謝您，先生。一共是兩千兩百八十元。

客人：兩千兩百八十元？我以為是兩千元。

出納員：嗯，帳單包括百分之四的稅金還有百分之十的服務費。

客人：我懂了。你們接受旅行支票嗎？

出納員：有的。可以請您在這簽名嗎？非常感謝您。我們很期待再度為您服務。

Word Bank 重要單字片語

1. add [æd] v. 添加；增加

Quiz 小試身手：請寫出正確英文單字

1. Your bill includes a 10% s_____ c_____ and a 5% t___ _____.

2. You don't have to pay any e_____ for t_____.
   您不用額外付稅。

答案：service, charge, tax, extra, tax

Methods of Payment 付款方式

Useful Expressions 常用的表達方法

cash	現金
credit card	信用卡
personal check	個人支票
traveler's check	旅行支票

出納員提問

問

1. How would you like to pay?

   請問您要以什麼方式付費？

2. How will you be paying?

   請問您要以什麼方式付費？

3. How would you like to make the payment?

   請問您要以什麼方式付費？

4. By which card would you like to pay?

   您要用哪種信用卡付帳？

5. In which currency will you be paying?

   您要用哪國貨幣付帳？

答

1. I'd like to pay by_____ . (personal check/traveler's check/ credit card) 我要用個人支票 / 旅行支票 / 信用卡來付帳。

2. I'll pay in _____ (cash/US dollars/NT dollars...)

我付現金／美元／台幣…。

3. I'll pay by _____ . (personal check/traveler's check/credit card)

我要用個人支票／旅行支票／信用卡來付帳。

客人詢問

問

Do you take/accept _____ (信用卡，如American Express, Visa...) / 旅行支票(traveler's check) / 外幣(foreign currency)) ？

答

1. Yes, we do.

2. I'm sorry, sir/ma'am. We don't accept _____ credit card/ foreign currency as payment.

我們不收 _____ 信用卡／外幣來付帳。

3. We don't honor traveler's check.

我們不接受旅行支票。

4. We don't accept personal check.

我們不接受個人支票。

信用卡付費

1. May I take a print of your card?

我幫您刷卡嗎？

2. I'm afraid they cannot extend the credit for the amount over the credit limit.

恐怕他們無法提高超過額度限制的金額。

帳單分配

1. Let's go Dutch!

   我們各自付帳吧！

2. Let's share the bill!

   讓我們平分帳款吧！

3. It's my treat!

   我請客！

4. Let me pick up the tab!

   讓我付帳吧！

Conversation 1 會話一

（*A cashier is asking about ways of payment.*）

Guest: I'd like to **settle** my bill.

Cashier: Here you are, sir. How would you like to pay for it?

Guest: I'll pay in US dollars.

Cashier: Thank you very much, sir.

Guest: That was a nice dinner.

（出納員正在詢問有關付款的方式。）

客人：我想要結帳了。

出納員：好的，先生，您的帳單。您要怎麼付費呢？

客人：我要用美金付費。

出納員：謝謝您，先生。

客人：這一頓晚餐真不錯。

Word Bank 重要單字片語

1. settle [ˋsɛtl] v. 支付；結算

大哉問：以美金而言，有哪些面額，英文怎麼說？	
dollar	元
dime	一角硬幣
fifty-cent piece	五角硬幣
half-dollar	五角硬幣
nickel	五分錢硬幣
cent	一分硬幣
quarter	二角五分硬幣

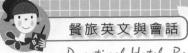

Conversation 2 會話二

(*A guest is going to settle the bill by traveler's check.*)

Guest: Do you accept traveler's check?

Cashier: I'm sorry, sir. We don't **honor** traveler's check as payment. Would you please pay with cash or pay by credit card?

Guest: That's OK. I'll pay by American Express. Do you accept that?

Cashier: Yes, of course, thank you very much.

(*The cashier **swipes** it.*)

Cashier: I'm terribly sorry, sir. The **system** doesn't accept your card. Would you like to try another one or pay by cash?

Guest: I don't have enough cash and I don't have another card, either.

Cashier: You can cash your traveler's check there. Or, if you are staying at our hotel, I can add the charge to your room bill and you could settle the bill upon when checking out.

Guest: That would be much better. I'm in room 1518.

（客人正準備用旅行支票付款。）

客人：你接受旅行支票嗎？

收納員：很抱歉，先生。我們不收旅行支票做為付款方式。請您用現金或是信用卡付款好嗎？

客人：沒關係。我用美國運通卡付費。你們接受嗎？

出納員：是的，非常感謝您。

（收納員刷卡。）

出納員：我非常抱歉，先生。這個系統不接受您的卡。您可以試另一張或是用現金付款嗎？

客人：我沒有足夠的現金，也沒有另一張卡。

出納員：您可以在那邊兌現你的旅行支票。或者，如果您有在旅館過夜，我可以將費用加到您的住宿帳單裡，那麼您就可以在退房時一併付費。

客人：那好多了。我在1518號房。

Word Bank 重要單字片語

1. honor [ˋɑnɚ] v. 承兌；支付

2. swipe [swaɪp] v. 碰擦；擦過

3. system [ˋsɪstəm] n. 系統

Quiz 小試身手：請寫出正確英文單字

Guest: Do you a_____ t_____'s check（旅行支票）?

Cashier: I'm sorry, sir. We don't h_____（承兌）traveler's
check a____（做為）payment. Would you please pay with
c_____（現金）or pay b_____ credit card?

答案：accept, traveler, honor, as, cash, by

Making Change/Receipts 找零與收據

Useful Expressions 常用的表達方法

客人需要收據時

1. Can I have a receipt?

   可不可以給我一張收據？

2. Can I have separate receipts for these?

   這些可不可以請你分開來開？

Conversation 1 會話一

(*A guest is asking for a receipt.*)

Guest: Can I have a **receipt**?

Cashier: Certainly, sir. May I have your company **invoice number**?

Guest: Sure, it's 232-5859.

Cashier: Here is your change, NT$250.

Guest: Thank you.

（客人要求開收據。）

客人：可以開張收據嗎？

收納員：當然可以，先生。我可以要您的公司統一編號嗎？

客人：好的，232-5859。

收納員：這是找您的零錢，兩百五十元。

客人：謝謝你。

Word Bank 重要單字片語

1. receipt [rɪ`sɪt] n. 收據
2. invoice [`ɪnvɔɪs] n. 發票；發貨單
3. invoice number n. phr. 統一編號

Conversation 2 會話二

(*A cashier is making change*.)

Cashier: How was everything tonight?

Guest: Good, thanks.

(*The guest hands the bill to the cashier*.)

Cashier: Thank you. That comes to NT$1,890.

Guest: Here you are.

Cahier: Out of NT$2000, and NT$110 is your change.

Guest: Thank you. Just **keep the change**.

（出納員正在找零。）

出納員：今晚一切都好嗎？

客人：很好，謝謝。

（客人把帳單遞給收納員。）

出納員：謝謝您。一共是一千八百九十元。

客人：給你。

出納員：收您兩千元，找您一百一十元。

客人：謝謝你，不用找了。

Word Bank 重要單字片語

1. Keep the change. 不用找了。（零錢你留著。）

Quiz 小試身手：請寫出正確英文單字

1. Guest: Can I have a r_____（收據）?

   Cashier: Certainly, sir. May I have your company i_____

   　　　　　number（統一編號）?

2. Cahier: Out of NT$1000, and NT$80 is your change.

   Guest: Thank you. K_____ t_____ c_____ .（不用找了）

答案：receipt, invoice, Keep, the, change

Exchanging Foreign Currency 換外幣

Useful Expressions 常用的表達方法

出納員

1. What currency do you have?

   請問您有什麼貨幣呢？

2. You would like to change _____NT$10000 into

   _____您想要把_____換成_____。

3. It comes to _____ at today's exchange rate.

   照今天的匯率，總共是_____。

Conversation 會話

(*A guest wants to exchange foreign currency.*)

Cashier: I'm afraid we don't accept foreign **currency**. Would you **exchange** it at the Cashier's Desk, please?

Guest: I see. Thank you.

Cashier's Desk: Good morning, sir. May I help you?

Guest: Yes, I'd like to exchange some money.

Cashier's Desk: Certainly, sir. What currency do you have?

Guest: NT dollars. I want to **convert** my NT dollars into US dollars.

Cashier's Desk: Sure, could you fill out this form, please?

Guest: I see.

(*After the guest fills in the form...*)

Guest: Here you are.

Cashier's Desk: Thank you, sir. You would like to change NT$10000 into US dollars. Is that correct?

Guest: Yes, that's correct.

Cashier's Desk: Just a moment, please. Thanks for your waiting, sir. It comes to US$330 at today's exchange rate.

Guest: I see. Thank you.

（客人想要換外幣。）

出納員：恐怕我們不收外幣。請您在收納員櫃檯那邊換外幣好嗎？

客人：我知道了。謝謝你。

出納櫃檯：早安，先生。我可以為您效勞嗎？

客人：是的，我想要換一點錢。

出納櫃檯：當然可以，先生。請問您有什麼貨幣呢？

客人：台幣。我想把我的一萬元台幣換成美金。

出納櫃檯：當然好，可以請您填這個表格嗎？

客人：我懂了。

（在客人填完表格之後…）

客人：給你。

收納櫃檯：謝謝您，先生。您想把您的一萬元台幣換成美金。對嗎？

客人：是的。

收納櫃檯：請稍待片刻。謝謝您的等待。照今天的匯率，總共是
三百三十元美金。

客人：我懂了，謝謝你。

Word Bank 重要單字片語

1. currency [ˋkɝənsɪ] n. 貨幣

2. exchange [ɪksˋtʃendʒ] v. 交換；兌換

3. convert [kənˋvɝt] v. 轉換

Quiz 小試身手：請寫出正確英文單字

1. 外匯率：＿＿＿＿＿＿＿＿＿

2. 貨幣：＿＿＿＿＿＿＿＿＿

3. 交換；轉換：e＿＿＿＿＿＿＿ / c＿＿＿＿＿＿＿

答案：exchange rate, currency, exchange/convert

Check-out 退房付費

Useful Expressions 常用的表達方法

詢問住房是否滿意

1. How was your stay?

   您住房愉快嗎？

2. Was everything satisfactory?

   一切都還滿意嗎？

問房號及留下鑰匙

1. What room were you in?

   您在哪個房間？

2. I'll just need your room keys, please.

   請給我您的房間鑰匙就好了。

3. May I have your room key, please?

   請給我您的房間鑰匙好嗎？

確認行李是否都已搬下來

1. Is all your baggage down already, sir?

   您所有的行李都已經搬下來了嗎，先生？

2. Have your bags been brought down already?

   您所有包包都已經帶下來了嗎？

問是否有額外的消費

1. Did you consume any beverages in the bar?

   您有在吧台消費任何飲料嗎？

2. Did you eat in any restaurants in our hotel during your stay?

   在住房期間，您有在我們飯店餐廳用餐嗎？

未在時間內辦理退房

1. Our check-out time is _____ (例：11. a. m.) but you used the room until _____ (例：3. p.m.)

   我們的退房時間是 _____（早上十一點）但您使用房間直到 _____（下午三點）。

2. I'm afraid there is additional charge for late check-outs.

   因為延遲退房，恐怕得付額外的費用。

Conversation 會話

（*A guest is checking out*.）

Cashier: Good morning, sir. May I help you?

Guest: Yes, I'd like to check out of room 309, please.

Cashier: Certainly, sir. Was everything **pleasing**?

Guest: Yes, It was fine.

Cashier: Did you eat in any of the restaurants this morning?

Guest: No, I didn't.

Cashier: Could you leave the key with us after your bags have been **brought** down, please?

Guest: Sure. Here you are.

Cashier: Just a moment, please. I'll prepare the bill for you. Thank you for waiting, sir. The bill comes to NT$5,420.

Guest: Thank you.

Cashier: And how will you be paying for this?

Guest: By cash, please. Here you are.

Cashier: Thank you, sir. Here is your change of NT$580. Could you please check it?

（客人正在辦理退房。）
出納員：早安，先生。我可以為您效勞嗎？
客人：是的，我想要退309號房，謝謝。
出納員：當然好，先生。一切都還滿意嗎？
客人：是的，不錯。
出納員：您今天早上有在任何餐廳吃飯嗎？
客人：不，我沒有。

出納員：可以請您在行李都帶下來之後，把鑰匙留給我們嗎？

客人：當然可以，給你。

出納員：請稍待片刻。我將為您準備帳單。謝謝您的等待。帳單一共是五千四百二十元。

客人：謝謝。

出納員：您要怎麼付費呢？

客人：用現金。請拿去。

出納員：謝謝您，先生。這是找您的錢，五百八十元。請您確認一下好嗎？

Word Bank 重要單字片語

1. pleasing [`plizɪŋ] adj. 令人愉快的；合意的；使人滿意的
2. bring [brɪŋ] v. 帶來；拿來（過去式為brought）

Quiz 小試身手：請寫出正確英文單字

Guest: I'd like to s_____ my bill.

Cashier: Certainly, sir. Could you f_____ your room number and
s_____（簽名）here, please?

Cashier: Thank you, sir. May I see the room key, please?

Guest: Sure. H_____y_____a_____ .（給你）

Cashier: It's Room #670. Thank you, sir.

答案：settle, fill, sign, Here, you, are

Thanks for Coming 道謝與送客

Useful Expressions 常用的表達方法

1. Please come again.

   請再度光臨。

2. Thanks for coming.

   謝謝光臨。

3. Enjoy the rest of your holiday.

   好好享受接下來的假期。

4. Have a safe trip home.

   祝您回程平安。

Conversation 1 會話一

（*A cashier is saying goodbye to guests and welcoming them back to the hotel*.）

Cashier: Thank you for **staying** at our hotel. I hope you enjoyed your stay.

Guest:　It was great. Thank you very much. We'll be back next time.

（出納員正在歡送客人並歡迎他們再度來訪。）

出納員：謝謝您在我們飯店住房。希望您住房愉快。

客人：很棒。非常謝謝你。下次我們會再回來。

Word Bank 重要單字片語

1. stay [ste] n. 停留；逗留

Conversation 2 會話二

(*A cashier is expressing **gratitude** to a leaving guest.*)

Cashier: Thanks for your coming. Did you enjoy your meal?

Guest:　Yes, it was delicious. We'll come back here soon.

（出納員正在對一個要離開的客人表達感激。）

收納員：謝謝您的光臨。您享受您的餐點嗎？

客人：是的，很好吃。我們很快會再來這裡。

Word Bank 重要單字片語

1. gratitude [ˋgrætəˌtjud] n. 感激之情；感恩；感謝

Quiz 小試身手：請寫出正確英文單字

1. Enjoy the r_____ of your h_____.
   好好享受接下來的假期。

2. Have a s_____ trip h_____.
   祝您回程平安。

答案：rest, holiday, safe, home

Extension 延伸學習：客房服務費用說明

情境會話

(*This is a conversation between a guest and Room Service when the guest is paying the* **bill**.)

Guest: I'd like to pay in cash.

Room Service: Certainly, sir. Please pay the Room Service waiter when he delivers your meal. You may use a meal voucher for Room Service but if your order **exceeds** the **value** of the voucher, could you pay the **difference**, please?

Guest: Sure.

Room Service: After **deducting** NT$500 from the value of the voucher, your dinner will be NT$925 including tax and **service charges**. We would like to bring the change when we deliver your meal. Which **denomination** of bill will you be paying with?

Guest: Well, I only have a NT$1,000 bill.

Room Service: OK. We will bring the **change** with your order.

（當客人要付款時，客人與客房服務員間的對話。）

客人：我想要付現。

客房服務：先生，當然可以。請將客房服務的費用，在服務生送餐時付費。您可以用客房服務的餐卷，但如果您的餐點超過餐卷的面額，可以請您補差額嗎？

客人：當然沒問題。

客房服務：在扣除餐卷的五百元之後，您的晚餐是九百二十五元，包括稅金及服務費。我們將在送餐的時候帶零錢給您。請問您會用什麼面額的貨幣呢？

客人：我只有一千元鈔票。

客房服務：好的，我們將會在送餐時找您零錢。

---

1. exceed [ɪk`sid] v. 超出

2. value [`vælju] n. 價值；面額

3. difference [`dɪfərəns] n. 差距；差額

4. deduct [dɪ`dʌkt] v. 扣除；減除

5. service charge n. phr. 服務費

6. denomination [dɪˌnɑmə`neʃən] n. （貨幣等的）面額

7. bill [bɪl] n. [美] 鈔票

8. change [tʃendʒ] n. 零錢

Multiple Choice 單一選擇題

1. I'm running out of _____ . Can I pay by credit card?

   (A) change (B) tip (C) cash (D) charge

2. A: It's NT $965, ma'am.

   B: OK. Here is $35. And keep the _____ .

   (A) change (B) check (C) tip (D) rate

3. I have a good time having dinner here. The service is great. I'd like

   to _____the waitress.

   (A) exchange (B) charge (C) tip (D) coin

4. We usually say "Could I have my bill, please?" to a _____ .

   (A) client (B) cashier (C) valet (D) bellhop

5. You should make sure you are given a _____ for

   everything you buy.

   (A) number (B) currency (C) ticket (D) receipt

6. Every citizen must pay _____.

   (A) tip (B) taxes (C) service charge (D) dollar

7. After we finished our dishes, John asked the waiter for the

   _____.

   (A) steak (B) bill (C) travel check (D) credit card

8. Cashier: Cash or credit card?

   Eason: _____, please. Here's my Visa Card.

(A) Cash (B) Both (C) Neither (D) Credit card

9. Grace: Here's my credit card.

Cashier: Thank you, sir. _____

(A) Will you leave a tip?

(B) Just a moment, please.

(C) Let's share the bill.

(D) Your card was not accepted.

10. Mandy: Your service is very good. I enjoy my dinner very much.

Cashier: Thank you, ma'am. _____

Mandy: I surely will.

(A) Do you have a good time?

(B) How would you like to pay?

(C) Would you like to wait for a while?

(D) Please come again and invite your friends here.

11. It's comes to NT$660, including the service _____.

(A) exchange (B) tip (C) charge (D) cash

12. It's time to go now. Let's _____ the check.

(A) settle (B) buy (C) clean (D) pray

13. Cashier: Here is your credit card receipt, sir. _____

Peggy: Would you please give me a pen?

Cashier: Sure, here you are.

(A) Please sign here.

(B) Please give me a pen.

(C) Please leave a tip.

(D) Please give me a hand,

14. Cashier: It is NT$2,420 all together, please.

　　Linda: Wait a minute—that's not right. It should be NT$2,200.

　　Cashier: Oh, it's correct, sir. _____

　　(A) I'm terribly sorry.

　　(B) You can pay in cash.

　　(C) Money is anything.

　　(D) A 10% service charge is added to the bill.

15. Henry: Please check the bill.

　　Waiter:_____, sir.

　　Henry: I'll pay in cash.

　　(A) How are you doing?

　　(B) How is the dinner?

　　(C) How will you be paying?

　　(D) What's going on?

16. Cashier: _____ Do you have another card?

　　Jody: No, I don't, but I have some cash.

　　(A) Please get out of here.

　　(B) Here is your receipt.

　　(C) Thank you, ma'am.

　　(D) Your credit card was not accepted.

17. Waiter: Here is your bill, ma'am. Please let me know when you
        are ready.

    Kim: _____ .

    Waiter: Thank you, ma'am. I'll be back right away with your
        change and receipt.

    (A) What's your problem?

    (B) I'll definitely come again.

    (C) Here you go.

    (D) How about a cup of coffee?

18. Andy: The meal is excellent. Let me pick up the tab.

    Irene: No, _____

    (A) I'll give you a discount.

    (B) It's my treat!

    (C) you should pay the bill.

    (D) it will be my pleasure.

19. Sharon: Excuse me, sir. May we have the check, please?

    Waiter: _____.

    (A) How are you.

    (B) Here you are.

    (C) Here comes the bus.

    (D) What a pity.

20. Judy: Let me pick up the tab.

    Eunice: No, _____.

Judy: OK, if you insist.

（選錯的）

(A) let's split the check.

(B) let's share the bill.

(C) let's go Dutch.

(D) it's my treat.

答案： (C)(A)(C)(B)(D)(B)(B)(D)(B)(D)

　　　(C)(A)(A)(A)(C)(D)(C)(B)(B)(B)

Announcements and Broadcasts

10 宣布與廣播服務

 本章摘要

Hotel and Cabin Announcements 廣播用語與事情宣布

Tour Guide 出發、抵達與集合時間地點說明

Emergency Announcements 地震、火災、停電等緊急狀況說明

Extension 延伸學習

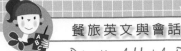
Introduction 學習重點

　　宣布與廣播服務時，要能短時間內準確並精簡的傳遞重要訊息。本章將介紹在餐廳、飯店、飛機上的廣播與事項宣布，還有導遊或領隊在出發、抵達、與集合時間說明，以及地震、火災、停電等緊急狀況說明等等。其中出發、抵達、與集合時間說明，是第一章時間的說明的延伸應用。

Useful Words 常用字彙

page	呼叫
announce	宣布
broadcast	廣播
emergency	緊急狀況
Contact	與…聯繫 / 聯絡

Hotel and Cabin Announcements 廣播用語與事情宣布

Useful Expressions 常用的表達方法

廣播的一般用語

Paging for Mr. / Mrs. / Miss＿＿＿＿＿＿ of Room ＿＿＿＿＿＿,

you have a_____(visitor/telephone). Please contact with
_____(Front Desk/operator). Thank you.

房號_____的_____先生／太太／小姐，您有_____（訪客／電
話），請與_____（櫃檯／總機）聯絡，謝謝！

客人

1. I need to page someone.

   我需要呼叫某人。

2. I'd like to speak to _____.

   我想要跟_____說話。

3. Hi, I think you are paging me.

   嗨，我想你們正在呼叫我。

4. Hello, I'm _____. You paged me.

   哈囉，我是_____。 你們剛剛有呼叫我。

5. Can you announce this for me?

   您能幫我播音這個嗎？

前櫃接待員

1. How do you spell his name, please?

   請問他的名字怎麼拼？

2. Could you give me a brief description?

   您能給我一個簡要的敘述嗎？

3. I'll page him for you.

   我將會為您呼叫他。

4. We'll make the announcement right now.

   我們將馬上為您廣播。

Conversation 會話

（*A caller is calling for contacting with her friend in a hotel restaurant.*）

Caller: Hello. Is this Moon Hotel?

Waiter: Yes. May I help you?

Caller: Yes, I'd like to speak to Ms. Lin, please. She should be in the restaurant having dinner now.

Waiter: How do you spell her name, please?

Caller: J.E.N.N.I.F.E.R, Jennifer.

Waiter: Thank you, ma'am. Could you give me a **brief description** about her?

Caller: She's about 25 years old, short with strait hair and wears glasses.

Waiter: Would you please hold the line? I'll **page** her for you.

(Broadcast) Paging for Ms. Jennifer Lin, you have a telephone call. Please **contact** with Front Desk. Thank you.

（一個人打電話來要與在飯店餐廳的朋友聯繫。）
打電話的人：哈囉，這裡是月神飯店嗎？
服務生：是的。我可以為您效勞嗎？

打電話的人：是的，請幫我接林女士。她現在應該在餐廳用晚餐。

服務生：請問她的名字怎麼拼？

打電話的人：J.E.N.N.I.F.E.R，珍妮佛。

服務生：謝謝您，女士。您可以簡單描述一下她嗎？

打電話的人：她大約25歲，短直髮，且戴眼鏡。

服務生：請您在線上稍候好嗎？我幫您廣播。

（廣播）珍妮佛・林女士，您有電話。請與櫃檯聯絡。謝謝您。

Word Bank 重要單字片語

1. brief [brɪf] adj. 簡略的；簡短的

2. description [dɪ`skrɪpʃən] n. 描寫；敘述

3. page [pedʒ] v.（在公共場所）喊叫尋找；廣播叫（人）

4. contact [`kɑntækt] v. 聯絡

Announcement 1 宣布事項一

（*Check-in baggage announcement.*）

Check-in baggage is required to hand to the driver either on the night before boarding, or by 8:00 am the next morning.

（宣布托運行李的事項）

托運行李必需要在登機前一晚或當天早上八點前集中交給司機。

Announcement 2 宣布事項二

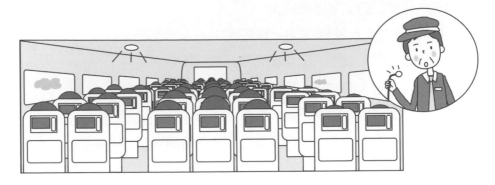

（*Cabin announcement*）

Welcome aboard Moon Airlines.

On behalf of Moon Airlines Captain Jennifer and her crew welcome you aboard. Our flight to Thailand will take approximately three hours. Let us remind you to fasten your seat belts, straighten your seats, and kindly refrain from smoking during take-off.

Under your seat there is a life vest like this one for each of you.

An oxygen mask will come down from overhead in case of an emergency.

Please press the call button whenever you need any help.

（機艙廣播）

歡迎搭乘月神航空。

機長珍妮佛及全體機員謹代表月神航空歡迎您搭乘本機。本班機飛抵泰國約需三小時。在此提醒在起飛過程中請您繫好安全帶，豎直椅背，還有請勿吸菸。

在各位的座位底下每人各有一件像這樣的救生衣。

若發生緊急情況，頭頂上會放下一只氧氣罩。

有任何需要時，請按呼叫鈕。

Quiz 小試身手：請寫出正確英文單字

1. 廣播叫人 v.：＿＿＿＿＿＿

2. 宣布 n.：＿＿＿＿＿＿＿

3. 聯繫 v.：＿＿＿＿＿＿

4. 緊急狀況 n.：＿＿＿＿＿＿

答案：page, announcement, contact, emergency

Tour Guide 出發、抵達與集合時間地點說明

Useful Expressions 常用的表達方法

1. We will be leaving in ＿＿＿＿＿＿＿(e.g. ten minutes...).

   我們將會在…後離開。

2. Please (double-)check your personal bag.

   請（再度）確認個人包包。

3. Please bring your personal property/belongings with you.

   請隨身攜帶個人財物。

4. We will gather together here ＿＿＿＿＿＿＿＿(e.g. in front of
   the JK Hotel) ＿＿＿＿＿＿＿(e.g. at 8:30a.m.).

   我們將會在這裡集合。

Announcement 1 宣布事項一

(*A tour guide is broadcasting*.)

We will be leaving in five minutes. Please check your bags and all your personal **property**, and remember to take them with you. The bus ride to your hotel will take about thirty minutes.

(導遊正在廣播。)

我們將再五分鐘之後離開。請確認您的行李以及所有個人財物，且記得帶走。到飯店的車程大約三十分鐘。

Word Bank 重要單字片語

1. property n. [`prapɚtɪ] n. 財產；資產；所有物

Announcement 2 宣布事項二

(*A tour guide is broadcasting*.)

We will arrive in the National Palace Museum at 3:30 p.m. Please bring your personal **belongings** with you and make sure that everyone gets a ticket from me.

(導遊正在廣播。)

我們將會在下午三點半到達國立故宮博物院。請帶好您的個人物品，並請每個人務必跟我拿一張門票。

Word Bank 重要單字片語

1. belongings [bə`lɔŋɪŋz] n. 財產;攜帶物品

Announcement 3 宣布事項三

(*A tour guide is broadcasting.*)

We will **gather** together here in front of the National Palace Museum at 5:30 p.m. Please be here **on time** so that we can have dinner before 6:30 p.m. If you have any problem when **visiting** the museum, please contact me at 0900-000-999.

(導遊正在廣播。)

我們將在下午五點半,在國立故宮博物院前集合。請準時到達,我們才能在晚上六點半前用晚餐。如果您在參觀博物館時有任何問題,請打0900-000-999與我連絡。

Word Bank 重要單字片語

1. gather [`gæðɚ] v. 集合
2. on time prep. phr. 準時
3. visit [`vɪzɪt] v. 參觀

Announcement 4 宣布事項四

(*A tour guide is broadcasting.*)

We're going to be pulling up to the hotel in just a few minutes. I hope that you **remain** in your seats until we have come to a

complete stop. Please **double check** to make sure your bag has been taken off the bus. I hope to see you tomorrow at 9:00 a.m. at the lobby.

（導遊正在廣播。）

我們的車子將在幾分鐘之後停在飯店。我希望您保持在座位上，直到我們已經完全停止。請重複確認您的包包已經拿下車子。明天早上九點我們在飯店大廳見。

Word Bank 重要單字片語

1. remain [rɪ`men] v. 保持；仍是
2. complete [kəm`plit] adj. 完整的；全部的
3. double check v. phr. 仔細的檢查

Quiz 小試身手：請寫出正確英文單字

1. 所有物: p_____
2. 個人物品: b_____
3. 集合: g_____
4. 仔細的檢查: d_____ c_____

答案：property, belongings, gather, double check

Emergency Announcements
地震、火災、停電等緊急狀況說明

Useful Expressions 常用的表達方法

地震

1. Be aware of falling objects and protect your head.

   注意墜落物，並保護您的頭部。

2. Please stay calm, keep away from windows, and get under a solid table in your room.

   請保持冷靜，遠離窗戶，且躲在房間內的桌子底下。

火災

1. The fire is out/under control.

   火已經撲滅了／在控制中。

2. Cover your nose and mouth with a wet towel in order not to inhale smoke.

   用濕毛巾掩住口鼻，以防吸入煙。

3. The fire extinguisher is put at the end of the hallway of each floor.

   滅火器被放在每層樓走廊的盡頭。

停電

1. Please follow the emergency light.

   請跟著緊急照明燈。

2. We'll use the emergency power right now and the power failure will be repaired very soon.

   我們將馬上使用緊急電源，停電的狀況將很快就修復。

疏散

1. Please leave your baggage behind and leave the hotel.

   請把行李留下並離開飯店。

2. Please follow the emergency exit door and withdraw this building immediately.

   請立刻從安全門（緊急逃生出口）離開房間。

Announcement 1 宣布事項一

（*Earthquake*）

May I have your attention, please? There has been a small earthquake. Please follow the emergency instructions broadcast throughout the hotel. Be aware of falling objects and protect your head. It's dangerous to go outside now. Please stay calm, keep away from windows, and get under a solid table in your room. Our hotel has a flexible earthquake-proof structure. Don't worry! It's quite safe inside your room. Thank you for your cooperation.

（地震）

各位先生女士請注意，現在有一點小地震。請遵守旅館播放的緊急指示。注意墜落物，並保護您的頭部。現在到外面很危險。請保持冷靜，遠離窗戶，且躲在房間內的桌子底下。本飯店有柔韌的防震構造。請勿擔心！在您的房間裡面很安全。謝謝您的合作。

Announcement 2 宣布事項二

（*Fire*）

Attention, please. There has been a small fire in the hotel. Please do not use the elevators. They are not in service. Crawl along the wall, and proceed towards an emergency staircase. The emergency exit is at the end of the hall way of each floor. Please keep calm and follow our hotel managers. Thank you for your cooperation.

（火災）

請注意。飯店裡有小火災。請不要使用電梯。電梯沒有在運作了。沿著牆壁爬行，並朝著緊急安全梯前進。緊急出口在每一樓走廊的尾端。請保持冷靜，跟隨我們飯店經理。謝謝您的合作。

Announcement 3 宣布事項三

（*A Blackout*）

May I have your attention, please? There is a blackout in our hotel. Please follow the emergency light. Don't panic! We'll use the emergency power right now and the power failure will be repaired very soon.

（停電）

各位先生女士請注意。飯店現在停電。請跟個緊急照明燈。不要恐慌！我們將馬上使用緊急電源，停電的狀況將很快就修復。

Quiz 小試身手：請寫出正確英文單字

1. 墜落物品: f_____ o_____

2. 緊急照明: e_____ l_____

3. 防震的結構：e_____-_____ s_____

答案：falling objects, emergency light, earthquake-proof struture

Extension 延伸學習：在飛機上

飛機上的人員及設備

（詳情請見第十四章）

announcement	機內廣播
take-off	起飛
captain	機長
crew	全體機員
pilot	駕駛員
purser	座艙長
flight attendant	空服員（空少或空姐）
air turbulence	空中亂流
air speed	飛行速度
altitude	高度
flying time	飛行時間
call button	呼叫鈕
oxygen mask	氧氣罩
aircraft	飛機

在飛機上遇到亂流時

Ladies and gentlemen:
We will be passing through turbulence/turbulent air. For your own safety, please remain seated and fasten your seat belts. Thank you.

各位先生女士：
我們即將經過一段不穩定的氣流，為了各位的安全，請留在座位上，將安全帶繫好。謝謝。

Multiple Choice 單一選擇題

1. She was _____ at the department store and told to go home.

   (A) announced (B) paged (C) arrived (D) blamed

2. Is the _____ exit suitable for disabled people?

   (A) emergency (B) light (C) hallway (D) floor

3. Give me a brief _____ of your purse.

   (A) invitation (B) speaking (C) description (D) imagination

4. I want to _____ with my old friends.

   (A) repair (B) describe (C) contact (D) announce

5. Power lines were cut down and we had a _____ for almost five hours.

   (A) earthquake (B) black-out (C) light (D) turbulence

6. On September 21st, a terrible _____ hit Taiwan. A lot of people was killed.

   (A) failure (B) trouble (C) black-out (D) earthquake.

7. The captain was making an important _____ now.

   (A) announcement (B) appointment (C) assignment (D) agreement

8. When will the bus _____?

   (A) broadcast (B) arrive (C) get (D) page

9. Everyone has the responsibility to _____ our environment.

  (A) pass (B) withdraw (C) protect (D) control

10. Please _____ the call button if there is an emergency.

  (A) pull (B) pay (C) hit (D) press

11. _____ There is a blackout in our hotel. Please follow the emergency light.

  (A) Be aware of falling objects!

  (B) We will arrive in the airport at 5:30 p.m.

  (C) May I have your attention, please?

  (D) May I help you?

12. Please follow the emergency instructions broadcast throughout the hotel. In addition, please keep calm and follow our hotel managers. _____

  (A) May I have your attention, please?

  (B) Thank you for your cooperation.

  (C) We're sorry for the carelessness.

  (D) Enjoy your meal!

13. May I have your attention, please? _____ Keep away from windows and protect your head.

  (A) There has been a small earthquake.

  (B) We will be passing through turbulence.

  (C) The elevator is going up.

  (D) The fire is under control.

14. _____ Please check all your personal properties.

The bus ride to the airport will take about twenty minutes.

(A) We will arrive at the airport in thirty minutes.

(B) We will be paying in cash.

(C) We will be leaving in ten minutes.

(D) We'll use the emergency power.

15. (Broadcast) Paging for Mr. Kyle Wang, your wife is looking for

you. _____Thank you.

(A) We're pulling up to the hotel.

(B) Please remain seated and fasten your seat belts.

(C) The power failure will be repaired in less than twenty minutes.

(D) Please contact with the Front Desk.

答案： (B)(A)(C)(C)(B)(D)(A)(B)(C)(D)
(C)(B)(A)(C)(D)

Talking about Weather

11 天氣說明

 本章摘要

Describing Weather 氣候說明

Describing Temperature 氣溫說明

Describing Clothing 衣著說明

Extension 延伸學習

Introduction 學習重點

　　出門旅遊，天氣是很重要的一環。出國旅行，了解當地氣候相當重要。到了當地，氣溫及衣著的說明，讓旅客能穿對衣服，不怕生病感冒，好好的享受旅行。本章將針對氣候、氣溫、還有衣著的說明做介紹。

Useful Words 常用字彙

四季

spring	春
summer	夏
fall/autumn	秋
winter	冬

描述天氣常用的字

rainy	下雨的
stormy	暴風雨的
snowy	下雪的
foggy	起霧的
windy	起風的
breezy	微風的
cloudy	多雲的

sunny	有陽光的
warm	溫暖的
hot	熱的
cool	涼爽的
cold	寒冷的
dry	乾的
humid	潮濕的
damp	有濕氣的；潮濕的
mild	溫暖的；溫和的

Describing Weather 氣候說明

Useful Expressions 常用的表達方法

天氣怎麼樣？

1. How's the weather in _____ （地方）？

2. What's the weather like in _____ （地方）？

Conversation 1 會話一

(*Mary is talking to her friend, Michael, who comes from Canada*.)

Michael: How many **seasons** are there in Taiwan?

Mary: There are four.

Michael: What season is it now?

Mary: It's winter.

Michael: How's the weather in the south?

Mary: Taiwan is a small **island surrounded** by **oceans**. In summer, it's hot all around the island. In winter, the north is cold and humid, **while** the south keeps cool and dry.

Michael: How come there is a difference?

Mary: Because the north is **subtropical**, but the south is **tropical**. The **climates** are different.

（瑪莉正在跟來自加拿大的朋友麥克說話。）

麥克： 在台灣有幾個季節？

瑪莉： 有四個。

麥克：現在是哪個季節？

瑪莉： 冬季。

麥克：南部的天氣怎麼樣？

瑪莉：台灣是個被海洋圍繞的小島。在夏天，整個島都很熱。冬天時，北部又冷又濕，而南部卻保持涼爽與乾燥。

麥克： 為什麼有這個不同？

瑪莉： 因為北部是位於副熱帶的，但南部是位於熱帶的。氣候不同。

Word Bank 重要單字片語

1. season [`sizn̩] n. 季節

2. island [`aɪlənd] n. 島

3. surround [sə`raund] v. 圍；圍繞；圈住

4. ocean [`oʃən] n. 海洋；海

5. while [waɪl] conj. 而；然而

6. subtropical [sʌb`trɑpɪkl̩] adj. 副熱帶的

7. tropical [`trɑpɪkl̩] adj. 熱帶的

8. climate [`klaɪmɪt] n. 氣候

Conversation 2 會話二

(*A and B are talking about the weather in Hualien.*)

A: What's the weather like in Hualien?

B: It's raining.

A: Is there a **typhoon** coming?

B: I don't know, but the wind is quite strong.

A: What's the **weather forecast** for tomorrow?

B: It's going to be a cold and windy day.

（A和B正在談論花蓮的天氣。）

A: 花蓮天氣怎麼樣？

B: 正在下雨。

A: 有颱風要來嗎？

B: 我不知道，但風相當強。

A: 明天氣象報告怎麼說？

B: 明天會很冷而且起風。

Word Bank 重要單字片語

1. typhoon [taɪˋfun] n. 颱風

2. forecast [ˋfɔrˏkæst] n. 預報；預測

3. weather forecast n. phr. 氣象預報

Quiz 小試身手：請寫出正確英文單字

A: W_____'s the weather like there? 天氣怎麼樣？

B: It's h_____ and s_____. 很熱而且出太陽。

A: Oh! It's c_____ and s_____ here. 喔！這裡又冷又下雪。

答案：What, hot, sunny, cold, snowy

Describing Temperature 氣溫說明

Useful Expressions 常用的表達方法

攝氏、華氏的算法與讀法

Celsius 攝氏 = 5/9 (Fahrenheit華氏 - 32)

Fahrenheit 華氏 = 9/5 Celsius + 32

請利用上述公式，換算攝氏與華氏溫度

Celsius	Fahrenheit
1. _____degrees	77 degrees
0 degree	2. _____degrees
35 degrees	3. _____ degrees
4. _____ degrees	14 degrees

答案：1. 25 2. 32 3. 95 4. -10

句型一

What's the temperature?	氣溫幾度？
What's the Celsius scale?	攝氏幾度？
It's(about)_____ degrees _____ (Celsius/Fahrenheit)	大約（攝氏／華氏）_____度。

(sub-zero/minus 零下)

例句：

1. It's about twenty-eight degrees Celsius.

    大約攝氏二十八度。

2. It's eighty-three degrees Fahrenheit.

    華氏八十三度。

3. It's sub-zero/minus thirteen degrees Celsius.

    攝氏零下十三度。

句型二

The weather is getting _____(colder/cooler/warmer/hotter). 天氣漸漸開始變冷／涼／暖／熱。
The temperature goes _____(up/down). 氣溫升高／降低。
The weather starts to cool down/warm up. 天氣開始涼了／暖和起來。

例句：

1. The weather is getting colder in winter.

    冬天天氣漸漸變冷。

2. The temperature goes down in winter.

    冬天氣溫下降。

3. The weather starts to warm up today.

    今天天氣開始暖和起來。

Conversation 會話

(*Mary is talking to her friend, Michael, who comes from America.*)

Michael: What's the **temperature** in Taipei right now?

Mary: It's 20 degrees Celsius.

Michael: It's 35 degrees Fahrenheit here. It's about 2 degrees Celsius.

Mary: Wow! It's very cold!

（瑪莉正在跟來自美國的朋友麥克說話。）
麥克： 現在台北的氣溫怎樣？
瑪莉： 攝氏二十度。
麥克： 我這裡華氏三十五度。大約攝氏兩度。
瑪莉： 哇！那非常冷耶！

Word Bank 重要單字片語
1. temperature [ˋtɛmprətʃɚ] n. 氣溫

Quiz 小試身手：請寫出正確英文單字
1. The weather is getting w_____ in spring.
2. The temperature g_____ d_____ in December.
3. The weather starts to c_____ d_____ in October.

答案：warmer, goes down, cool down

Describing Clothing 衣著說明

Useful Expressions 常用的表達方法

衣著

T-shirt	運動
shorts/short pants	短褲
dress	洋裝
skirt	裙子
shirt	襯衫
swimsuits	泳衣
cap	棒球帽
sneakers	球鞋
high heels	高跟鞋
shoes	鞋子
sunglass	太陽眼鏡
sweater	毛衣
suit	西裝
jacket	夾克
coat	外套
jeans	牛仔褲
socks	襪子
boots	靴子
gloves	手套
scarf	圍巾
hat	帽子
raincoat	雨衣
umbrella	雨傘

Conversation 會話

(*A and B are talking about what to wear tomorrow*.)

A: I'm **wondering** what I should wear tomorrow.

B: The **weatherman** said it will be cold and rainy tomorrow.

A: Oh, really. Then I'm going to wear a sweater and a coat, along with boots.

B: Are you afraid of **getting a cold**?

A: Yes. Maybe I'll have to wear a scarf.

B: I think that will be enough.

（A和B正在談論明天的穿著。）

A：我正在想我明天要穿什麼。

B：氣象播報員說明天將會很冷且下雨。

A：喔，真的嗎。那我明天要穿毛衣、外套，跟靴子。

B：你很害怕會感冒嗎？

A：是的。也許我需要圍圍巾。

B：我想那應該夠了吧。

Word Bank 重要單字片語

1. wonder [ˋwʌndɚ] v. 納悶；想知道

2. weatherman [ˋwɛðɚmæn] n. 氣象預報員

3. get a cold v. phr. 感冒

Quiz 小試身手：請寫出正確英文單字

A: The w_____（氣象播報員）said it will be cold and rainy tomorrow.

B: Oh, really. Then I'm going to wear a s_____（毛衣）and a c_____（外套）, along with b_____（靴子）.

答案：weatherman, sweater, coat, boots

Extension 延伸學習：一週天氣預報

一週天氣預報圖是什麼樣子？要怎麼看天氣？

Issued :2007/12/05 16:30

Unit:℃

Valid :2007/12/06~2007/12/12

	12/07 Tue.	12/07 Fri.	12/08 Sat.	12/09 Sun.	12/10 Mon.	12/11 Tue.	12/12 Wed.
Taipei City	18~22	15~19	15~21	17~24	19~26	20~26	20~26
North Area	17~22	14~19	13~21	16~24	18~27	19~27	19~27
Central Area (Taichung, Changhua, Nantou, Yunlin、Chiayi)	16~24	15~24	13~25	14~27	16~28	18~28	18~28
South Area (Tainan, Kaohsiung, Pingtung)	18~26	16~26	15~27	16~29	18~30	19~30	19~30

	12/07 Tue.	12/07 Fri.	12/08 Sat.	12/09 Sun.	12/10 Mon.	12/11 Tue.	12/12 Wed.
North-East Area (Keelung, Yilan)	17~22	15~20	15~22	17~23	18~25	19~25	19~25
East Area (Hualien)	18~23	16~21	16~23	16~24	17~25	19~27	19~27
South-East Area (Taitung)	19~26	17~26	17~27	18~28	20~29	20~29	20~29
Penghu Area	19~26	19~26	19~26	19~26	19~26	19~26	19~26
Kinmen Area	19~26	19~26	19~26	19~26	19~26	19~26	19~26
Matsu Area	19~26	19~26	19~26	19~26	19~26	19~26	19~26

（資料來源：中央氣象局網站）

請根據上面的一週天氣預報,來說明天氣。

1. It's _____ and _____ in Taipei city on December 7th .

2. It's _____ and _____ in Nantou on on December 12th.

3. It's _____ and _____ in Matsu Area on Decomeber 8th.

4. It's about _____ to 30 degrees Celsius in _____ Area on December 11th.

5. It's about 12 to _____ degrees Celsius in _____ Area in December 7th.

答案:1. cool, rainy 2. hot, sunny 3. cool, cloudy 4. 19, South
      5. 15, Matsu

Keelung &
North Coast

Taipei City

Taoyuan Area

Taipei Area

Hsinchu Area

Matsu
Area

Miaoli Area

Yilan Area

Taichung Area

Kinmen
Area

Changhua Area

Nantou Area

Yunlin Area

Hualien Area

Chiayi Area

Penghu
Area

Tainan Area

Kaohsiung Area

Taitung Area

Kaohsiung City

Pingtung Area

Hengchun Peninsula

請根據以上一週天氣預報，說明氣溫的變化。

1. The weather is _____ _____ in North Area.

2. The temperature is _____ _____ in East Area.

3. The weather this week starts to _____ _____ in Taiwan.

答案：1. getting warmer 2. going up 3. warm up

Multiple Choice 單一選擇題

1. In Taiwan, it is usually hot and _____ in summer.

   (A) happy (B) cool (C) humid (D) cold

2. John was born in Taiwan on July 2nd. He was born in _____.

   (A) fall (B) summer (C) spring (D) winter

3. The _____ is low in the morning, but it is high in the evening.

   (A) temperature (B) degree (C) forecast (D) snow

4. Taiwan is a(n) _____. It is surrounded by sea.

   (A) ocean (B) season (C) island (D) mountain

5. It's _____ now, but according to the forecast, it will be rainy in the evening.

   (A) hot (B) breezy (C) foggy (D) sunny

6. Today is a _____ day. I can't see the road clearly when driving.

   (A) sunny (B) breezy (C) foggy (D) cloudy

7. Taiwan's _____ is hot and humid.

   (A) climate (B) humidity (C) island (D) temperature

8. In winter, it's _____ in Taipei, but it's dry in Kaohsiung.

   (A) snowy (B) mild (C) tropical (D) damp

9. In Taiwan, most of the _____ come in summer and fall .

   (A) seasons (B) typhoons (C) climates (D) earthquakes

10. Bananas are _____ fruit.

   (A) strong (B) winter (C) hot (D) tropical

11. Tommy: _____

   Jay: We can play basketball at 5 p.m.

   (A) It's cold today.

   (B) What a sunny day!

   (C) I hate rainy days.

   (D) The weather is getting colder and colder.

12. Jay: It's raining heavily outside. Oh, no!

   Tommy: _____

   (A) Yes, it's sunny.

   (B) You should wear a scarf.

   (C) You must bring an umbrella with you.

   (D) You have to put on your shorts.

13. Jay: The temperature is 77 degrees Fahrenheit now.

   Tommy: _____

   Jay: 25 degrees.

   (A) What season is it now?

   (B) Can you describe them?

   (C) What's the weather like?

   (D) What is that on the Celsius scale?

14. Jay: What's the weather like outside?

Tommy: It's a little cold. _____

（選錯的）

(A) Will you wear a scarf?

(B) You'd better wear short pants.

(C) You'd better wear long sleeves.

(D) You must wear a coat.

15. Tommy: _____

Jay: It's going to snow. You'd better stay at home.

(A) What's the climate in winter?

(B) What's the forecast for today?

(C) What's the temperature?

(D) What's the humidity?

答案：(C)(B)(A)(C)(D)(C)(A)(D)(B)(D)
　　　　(B)(C)(D)(B)(B)

Dealing with Complaints

12 抱怨的處理

 本章摘要

Introduction 學習重點

　　在飯店或餐廳服務客人時，常常會遇到客人抱怨。如何禮貌並有效的幫客人處理及應對，是餐旅服務業的必修學分。本章將針對各種可能情境做介紹，包括出菜太慢、上錯菜、菜中有異物、對餐具的抱怨、弄髒客人衣物、別的客人太吵、電器故障時、冷氣太冷或太弱時、飛機行程等延誤時該怎麼應對。

Useful Words 常用字彙

1. Change v. 換掉
2. move v. 移動

> I'll have it/you _____（動詞過去分詞）(right away/right now/at once). 我將會（馬上）立刻把它 / 幫您 _____.

例：I'll have it changed right away.

我將馬上把它換掉。

I'll have you moved to a quiet place.

我將幫您移到安靜一點的座位。

Waiting for Dishes 出菜太慢時

Useful Expressions 常用的表達方法

客人

1. I've asked for a glass of water quite a while ago.

   我之前就要求要一杯水了。

2. I ordered my meal at least 30 minutes ago and it still hasn't come.

   我至少三十分鐘前就點餐了，到現在還是沒來。

3. We've been waiting for our food for over 40 minutes. Why is it taking so long?

   我們等我們的食物已經超過四十分鐘了。為什麼要這麼久？

4. We've been here for over 20 minutes.

   我們已經在這超過二十分鐘了。

5. I ordered room service over 20 minutes ago, but I am still waiting for the food.

   我們二十分鐘前要求客房服務，但我們現在仍然在等。

6. Is there anything you can do to speed things up?

   你有沒有什麼方法可以讓我們的餐點快一點送上來的？

7. Do you have any idea how much longer it's going to take?

   你知道還要等多久嗎？

侍者

1. I'll check on your order immediately.

   我會立刻確認您的餐點。

2. I'm sorry. Today is a holiday, so we are really busy.

很抱歉。今天是假日所以我們真的很忙。

3. I'll have the kitchen put a rush on your order.

我會催促廚房加快您的餐點。

4. I'll check with the kitchen.

我會跟廚房確認一下。

Conversation 會話

(*A guest is complaining for the delay*.)

Guest: When will our table be ready? We've ordered our food over half an hour ago, and we're still waiting for it. **What's going on**?

Waiter: I'm very sorry, we are really busy tonight. I'll check with the kitchen and have it brought to you right away.

Guest: Thanks. I'll **appreciate** that. And please make it quick. I have an **appointment** in 20 minutes.

Waiter: Yes, I will.

(*After a few minutes, the waiter brings the order*.)

Waiter: I'm sorry for the delay. Please enjoy your meal.

（客人在抱怨延誤送餐。）

客人：我們的餐點什麼時候會準備好？我們半小時前就點餐了，現在卻還在等。怎麼回事呢？

服務生：很抱歉，我們今晚真的很忙。我會與廚房確認，並馬上送上您的餐點。

客人：謝謝。很感謝你。請快一點，我二十分鐘後有個約會。

服務生：是的，我會快一點。

（在幾分鐘之後，服務生把菜送上。）

服務生：很抱歉耽誤了您的餐點。祝您用餐愉快。

Word Bank 重要單字片語

1. What's going on? 發生了什麼事？

2. appreciate [ə´priʃɪ͵et] v. 感謝；感激

3. appointment [ə´pɔɪntmənt] n.（尤指正式的）約會

Quiz 小試身手：請寫出正確英文單字

1. Is there anything you can do to s_____ things ____（快一點）?

2. I'll h_____ the kitchen put a r_____ o_____ your order（加快您的餐點）.

答案：speed, up, have, rush, on

Wrong Order and Dishes 上錯菜時

Useful Expressions 常用的表達方法

客人

1. I ordered baked potato, not French fries.

   我點的是烤馬鈴薯，不是薯條。

2. I didn't order this.

   我沒有點這個。

3. I don't think this is not what I ordered.

   我不認為這是我點的東西。

4. You may have the wrong order.

   你可能點錯了。

5. May I speak with your manager, please?

   請問我可以跟你們經理談談嗎？

侍者

1. What did you order?

   您點了什麼？

2. You had the regular coffee, right?

   您點了一杯普通的咖啡，對嗎？

3. Let me get that out of your way. I'll be right back with the correct order.

   我來幫您收走，我馬上把正確的餐點端過來。

4. I'll bring your _____(soup/coffee/salad...) right away.

   我會馬上將您的_____（湯／咖啡／沙拉）送來。

5. Let me bring your＿＿＿＿＿＿(soup/coffee/salad...).

讓我送上您的＿＿＿＿＿＿＿（湯／咖啡／沙拉）。

Conversation 會話

(*When a waiter is serving the wrong meal*...)

Guest: Waiter! I didn't order this.

Waiter: I'm very sorry about that. What did you order?

Guest: I ordered a Beef Curry, not Shrimp Curry.

Waiter: I see, ma'am. I'll bring it to you **right** away.

(*After a few minutes, the waiter brings the right dish*.)

Waiter: Here is your Beef Curry. I'm very sorry for the wrong order.
　　　　Please enjoy your meal.

（當服務生上錯菜時…）

客人：服務生！我沒有點這個。

服務生：我很抱歉。您點了什麼？

客人：我的點是咖哩牛肉，不是咖哩蝦。

服務生：我知道了，女士。我馬上為您送上。

（幾分鐘之後，服務生送來正確的餐點。）

服務生：這是您的咖哩牛肉，很抱歉點錯餐點，祝您用餐愉快。

Word Bank 重要單字片語

1. right [raɪt] adj. 正確的；準確的

Quiz 小試身手：請寫出正確英文單字

1. You may have the w_____ o_____. 你可能點錯了。

2. Let me get that o_____ o_____ your way. I'll be right back
   w_____ the c_____(=right) order.

答案：wrong, order, out of, with, correct

Something Wrong with Dishes 菜中有異物時

Useful Expressions 常用的表達方法

客人

1. I'd like to speak with your manager.
   我想要跟你的經理談談。

2. Why is there an egg shell in my soup?
   為什麼我的湯裡會有蛋殼？

3. There is a lock of hair in my ice cream.
   我的冰淇淋裡有一根頭髮。

侍者

1. Let me get you another _____(bowl).
   我幫您換_____（一碗）。

2. I'll bring you a new _____(one/glass).

我將會幫您換新的_____（一個／一杯）。

Conversation 會話

（*When there is a fly in a guest's salad*...）

Guest: Waiter! There is a fly in my salad!

Waiter: I'm **terribly** sorry. I'll bring another one **at once**.

Guest: Make sure that there is no fly this time.

Waiter: That's for sure. I'll bring it to you in two minutes.

（當客人的沙拉裡有蒼蠅…）

客人：服務生！我的沙拉裡有蒼蠅。

服務生：真的很抱歉，我馬上送上另一份。

客人：這次要確定沒有蒼蠅了。

服務生：那是一定的。我會在兩分鐘後帶來給您。

Word Bank 重要單字片語

1. terribly [`tɛrəbḷɪ]【口】adv. 很；非常
2. at once 馬上；立刻

Quiz 小試身手：請寫出正確英文單字

1. 經理：m_____

2. 很；非常：t_____

答案：manager, terribly

Something Wrong with Tableware

對餐具的抱怨

Useful Expressions 常用的表達方法

1. The spoon is dirty.

   湯匙有點髒。

2. I dropped my fork.

   我叉子掉了。

3. Would you please give me another plate? This one is a little dirty.

　可以請你給我另一個盤子嗎？這個有點髒。

4. This glass has some lipstick on it.

　這玻璃杯上面有一些口紅印。

Conversation 會話

(*A guest is complaining about the knife.*)

Guest: Excuse me! The knife is not **sharp** enough.

Waiter: I'm sorry. I'll bring another one right away.

Guest: Thank you. And please make sure that it's also clean.

Waiter: Certainly. I'll be right back.

（客人在抱怨刀子。）

客人：不好意思！刀子不夠利。

服務生：我很抱歉。我馬上送上另一個。

客人：謝謝你。也請確認是否乾淨。

服務生：當然。我會馬上回來。

Word Bank 重要單字片語

1. sharp [ʃarp] adj. 鋒利的；尖的

Quiz 小試身手：請寫出正確英文單字

1. I d_____ my f_____.

   我叉子掉了。

2. This glass has some l_____（口紅印）on it.

答案：dropped, fork, lipstick

Staining 弄髒客人衣物時

Useful Expressions 常用的表達方法

侍者

1. Let me get a new towel for your clothes.

   讓我拿一個新的毛巾讓您擦衣服。

2. I'm very sorry for the mistake.

   我很抱歉犯了這個錯。

3. We will arrange for your clothes to be cleaned at once.

   我們會立刻將您的衣服送洗。

4. We can arrange a room for you where you can wait until your clothes are cleaned.

   我可以為您安排一間房間，您可以在那裡等到衣服洗乾淨。

5. It will be on the house/free/paid by the restaurant.

   那是免費／由餐廳付費的。

6. I'd like to apologize for our carelessness.

   我想為我們的疏忽道歉。

Conversation 1 會話一

(*A waiteress **accidentally spills** a cup of coffee on a guest.*)

Waiteress: Here is your coffee...Oops! I'm very sorry. I'll bring you a
clean towel to clean up immediately.

Guest: Please be hurry.

Head Waiter: I'm the Head Waiter. We are very sorry to have caused
you this trouble. May I clean it up for you?

Guest: No, I'll do it myself.

Head Waiter: Are you a hotel guest?

Guest: No. Why?

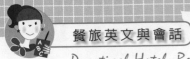
Head Waiter: If you could send us the bill for your laundry, we will pay for it.

Guest: I see.

Head Waiter: I'd like to apologize for our **carelessness** again.

（女服務生意外的將一杯咖啡灑在客人身上。）

女服務生：這是您的咖啡……啊！我很抱歉。我將會送上乾淨的毛巾，馬上清理。

客人：請快一點。

男性領班：我是領班。很抱歉造成您的麻煩。我可以為您清理嗎？

客人：不用了，我自己來。

男性領班：您是飯店房客嗎？

客人：不是。為什麼這麼問？

男性領班：如果您可以把洗衣帳單寄給我們，我們會為您付帳。

客人：我知道了。

男性領班：我想為我們的疏忽再次道歉。

Word Bank 重要單字片語

1. accidentally [͵æksə`dɛntl̩ɪ] adv. 偶然地；意外地

2. spill [spɪl] v. 使溢出；使濺出；使散落

3. carelessness [`kɛrlɪsnɪs] n. 粗心大意

Conversation 2 會話二

(*A waiter accidentally spills something on a guest*.)

Guest: Oh! It **spilt** all over my shirt...

Head Waiter: I'd like to apologize for this mistake. Are you a hotel guest?

Guest: Yes, I'm a hotel guest. Why?

Head Waiter: I'll have the housekeeping **dry-clean** your shirt for you. And we'll deliver your clothes as fast as we can. It's free of **charge**. Could you **accompany** me to your room and change clothes there?

Guest: OK, now I'll go up to my room and change.

Head Waiter: May I have your room number, please?

Guest: It's Room 1248.

（服務生不小心將食物或飲料濺在客人身上。）

客人：喔！都濺到我的襯衫上了。

領班：我為此感到很抱歉。您是飯店房客嗎？

客人：是的，我是飯店房客。為什麼這麼問？

領班：我會請房務為您乾洗您的襯衫。然後我們將儘快送回您的襯衫。是免費的。您可以跟我到您的房間，把衣服換下來嗎？

客人：好的，現在我就上去我房間換衣服。

領班：可以請問您的房號嗎？

客人：1248房。

Word Bank 重要單字片語

1. spilt [spɪlt] v. 濺（spill的過去式和過去分詞）

2. dry-clean [ˋdraɪˋklɪn] v. 乾洗（衣物）

3. accompany [əˋkʌmpənɪ] v. 陪同；伴隨

Quiz 小試身手：請寫出正確英文單字

1. We will a_____（安排）for your clothes to be c_____ a____ o_____（立刻）.

2. It will be o____ the h_____ (=free = p_____ by the restaurant).

3. I'd like to apologize for our c_____（疏忽）.

答案：arrange, cleaned, at once, on, house, paid, carelessness

Noisy Guests 別的客人太吵時

Useful Expressions 常用的表達方法

客人

1. The person next to my room has his TV turned on really loud.

   我隔壁房間的人把電視開得真的很大聲。

2. It's so noisy that I can't fall asleep.

   太吵了讓我睡不著。

3. People sitting besides us are speaking too loud.

   坐我旁邊的人講話太大聲了。

Conversation 會話

（*When other guests are too noisy...*）

Receptionist: Front desk. May I help you?

Guest: Yes, this is Room 1248. There seems to be a party going on in the room next to mine. It's very **noisy** and I can't sleep!

Receptionist：OK. I'll send someone up right away. We are very sorry for the inconvenience.

Guest: Thanks for your **efforts**.

Receptionist：You're welcome. Good night, sir.

（當其他客人太吵時…）

櫃檯人員：櫃檯。我可以為您效勞嗎？

客人：是的，這是1248號房。在我隔壁房間好像在舉行派對。 非常吵，吵到讓我無法入睡。

櫃檯人員：好的。我將馬上派人上去。很抱歉造成您的不便。

客人：謝謝你的幫忙。

櫃檯人員：不客氣。晚安，先生。

Word Bank 重要單字片語

1. noisy [`nɔɪzɪ] adj. 喧鬧的；嘈雜的
2. effort [`ɛfɚt] n. [U][C] 努力；盡力

Quiz 小試身手：請寫出正確英文單字

1. It's so n_____ that I can't fall a_____.

太吵了讓我睡不著。

2. People sitting b_____ us are speaking too l_____.
   坐我旁邊的人講話太大聲了。

答案：noisy, asleep, besides, loud

Something Wrong with Electric Appliances
電器故障時

Useful Expressions 常用的表達方法

The _____ (lamp/coffee maker) doesn't work.
這個 _____ （燈／咖啡機）壞了（無法正常運作）。

Conversation 會話

（*When the TV doesn't **work**...*）

Receptionist: Reception desk. May I help you?

Guest: The TV in my room doesn't seem to work.

Receptionist: I'm sorry, sir. I'll send someone to check for you and
fix it right away.

Guest: Thank you.

（當電視無法正常運作…）
櫃檯人員：櫃檯。請問我可以為您效勞嗎？

客人：我房間的電視似乎無法運作。

櫃檯人員：抱歉，先生。我將派人去為您確認，並馬上修理。

客人：謝謝你。

Word Bank 重要單字片語

1. work [wɜk] v. 運作
2. fix [fɪks] v. 修理

Quiz 小試身手：請寫出正確英文單字

Guest: The lamp in my room doesn't w_____（運作）.

Receptionist：I'm sorry, sir. I'll s_____（派遣）someone to

c_____（確認）for you and f___（修理）it at once.

答案: work, send, check, fix

Air-conditioning 冷氣太冷或太弱時

Useful Expressions 常用的表達方法

客人

1. The air-conditioner in my room is not cold enough.

   我房間的冷氣不夠冷。

2. There is no heat in my room.

   我的房間沒有暖氣。

Conversation 會話

(*When it is too hot or too cold...*)

Guest: Is this housekeeping?

Housekeeping: Yes, it is.

Guest: My room is too cold.

Housekeeping: Did you **adjust** the temperature?

Guest: Yes, I did, but it's still too cold.

Housekeeping: I'll send someone to check for you immediately.

（當太熱或太冷時…）

客人：是房務部嗎？

房務部：是的。

客人：我的房間太冷了。

房務部：客人：您有調整溫度嗎？

客人：有，我調整了，但還是太冷。

房務部：我馬上派人去為您確認。

Word Bank 重要單字片語

1. adjust [əˋdʒʌst] v. 調整

Quiz 小試身手：請寫出正確英文單字

1. 冷氣: a_____-c_____
2. 暖氣: h_____

答案：air-conditioner, heat

Delay 飛機行程等延誤時

Useful Expressions 常用的表達方法

1. We are sorry to announce that the flight is going to be
   _____(e.g. one hour) late because _____(e.g. we're
   loading late luggage).
   很抱歉我們必須宣布這個飛機將延誤_____（例如一小時），
   因為_____（例如正在裝載晚到的行李）。

2. We're very sorry for the delay/inconvenience.
   造成不便之處敬請見諒。

Conversation 會話

（*When the flight is delayed...*）

Passenger: Can you tell me about the **status** of my flight?

Clerk: Certainly. Which flight are you on?

Passenger: Moon Airlines 388.

Clerk: I'll check for you. Your flight will be delayed by two hours. We're very sorry for the delay.

Passenger: Thank you anyway.

（當班機被延誤時…）

乘客：你可以告訴我班機的現況嗎？

櫃檯人員：當然。您是搭乘哪個班機？

乘客：月神航空388班機。

櫃檯人員：我將為您確認。您的飛機將延遲兩小時。我們對此感到很抱歉。

乘客：無論如何，謝謝你。

Word Bank 重要單字片語

1. status [ˋstætəs] n. 情形，狀況

Announcement 宣布事項

Attention passengers on Moon Airlines 388 to New York. We are sorry to announce that the flight is going to be two hours late because we're loading late luggage. We'd like to apologize for this inconvenience.

請搭乘月神航空388班機到紐約的旅客注意。很抱歉我們必須宣布這個班機將延誤兩個小時，因為我們正在裝載晚到的行李。造成您的不便之處，敬請見諒。

Quiz 小試身手：請寫出正確英文單字

1. Can you tell me about the s_____（情況）of my f_____（班機）?

2. We're very sorry for the i_____（不便）.

答案：status, flight, inconvenience

Extension 延伸學習：帳單問題

當客人提出帳單問題時會怎麼說？該怎麼回答呢？

客人

1. There's something wrong with our bill. We didn't order any dessert.
   帳單有些問題。我們沒有點甜點。

2. There seems to be a mistake on this bill.
   帳單似乎有些錯誤。

3. I thought the coffee was on the house.
   我以為咖啡是免費的(由餐廳提供的)。

侍者

1. I'm sorry for that. I'll check for you right now.
   我很抱歉。我馬上為您確認。

2. Did you have any beverage?
   您有喝任何飲料嗎？

3. If you order the special meal for today, you can get a cup of coffee for free.
   如果您點今日特餐，您可以享用一杯免費咖啡。

Multiple Choice 單一選擇題

1. I _____ all the doors twice before I leave the hotel.

   (A) asked (B) checked (C) doubted (D) viewed

2. I'm sorry for my _____.

   (A) pleasure (B) charge (C) mistake (D) wrong

3. We'd like to apologize for any _____caused by the blackout.

   (A) manager (B) inconvenience (C) temperature (D) bill

4. He _____ his keys, and he picked them up.

   (A) ordered (B) gave (C) stopped (D) dropped

5. My plane will _____ about two hours.

   (A) delay (B) arrive (C) leave (D) adjust.

6. I can't get the television to _____.

   (A) leak (B) flush (C) work (D) order

7. We will offer the service for _____.

   (A) free (B) fun (C) bill (D) cheap

8. This room is so _____that we have to clean it.

   (A) expensive (B) small (C) dirty (D)bright.

9. We didn't mean to cause you any _____.

   (A) charge (B) accompany (C) trouble (D) arrival

10. Could you please _____ up the table for me?

    (A) wake (B) get (C) warm (D) clean

11. Henry: I'm not satisfied with the service here. _____

    Waiter: Just a moment, sir.

    (A) I had a great time here.

    (B) I ordered a garden salad.

    (C) I'd like to speak to the manager.

    (D) I'd like to have a cup of coffee.

12. Henry: Excuse me, I think the bill is wrong.

    Cashier: I'm sorry for the confusion, ma'am. _____

    Henry: I see. Thank you.

    (A) You need to pay in cash.

    (B) It's not my fault.

    (C) I think you are right.

    (D) We added a ten percent service charge to the bill.

13. Manager: I'm sorry for the mistake, ma'am. _____

    Dana: I'm afraid it's too late. I'll never come here again.

    (A) Would you please accept our apologies?

    (B) I'm disappointed at the food.

    (C) The service is not bad here.

    (D) I'll send someone to your room.

14. Henry: Excuse me. This is Room 525. The room is facing the
    main street and it's noisy. Besides, there doesn't seem to
    be heat in my room. _____

Receptionist: Certainly, let me check to see if there are any vacancies.

(A) Could you give me a pillow?

(B) Could you sign here, please?

(C) Could you change my room?

(D) Would you please hurry up?

15. Guest: This steak is rare, but I want it well-done.

Waitress: I'm really sorry for the mistake. _____

(A) I'll change your room soon.

(B) I'll be right back with the correct order.

(C) The charge will be added to your bill.

(D) The chef is new but great.

16. Guest: When will our table be ready? We've ordered our food over twenty minutes ago

Waiter: I'm very sorry for the delay, we are really busy tonight.

_____.

(A) I'll check the bill and give you a receipt right away.

(B) I'll check with the kitchen and have it brought to you right away.

(C) The coffee machine doesn't work.

(D) I'll appreciate it.

17. Waiter: Here is your juice... Oops! I'm terribly sorry, sir.

_____

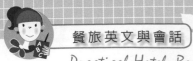

Dana: Please hurry up.

(A) I'll bring your order right away.

(B) I'll treat you another coffee.

(C) I'll bring you a clean towel immediately.

(D) I'll keep the change.

18. Guest: My room is too hot.

    Housekeeping: _____

    Guest: Yes, I did, but it's still too hot. .

    (A) Did you enjoy your stay?

    (B) Did you make a reservation?

    (C) Did you adjust the temperature?

    (D) Did you have any beverage?

19. Passenger: Would you please tell me about the status of my
        flight?

    Clerk: Certainly. Which flight are you on?

    Passenger: Joon Airlines 292.

    Clerk: I'll check for you._____ We'd like to apologize
        for the delay.

    Passenger: Thank you anyway.

    (A) We can arrange a room for you.

    (B) We're passing through turbulence.

    (C) The light is on.

    (D) Your flight will be delayed one hour.

20. Dana: _____ This one is a little dirty.

Waitress: Certainly, ma'am.

(A) Would you please give me another fork?

(B) Could you do me a favor?

(C) It's so noisy that I can't fall asleep.

(D) Will it be on the house?

答案：(B)(C)(B)(D)(A)(C)(A)(C)(C)(D)

(C)(D)(A)(C)(B)(B)(C)(C)(D)(A)

 *Travel*

13 旅遊

 本章摘要

Sightseeing 安排旅遊景點
Making a Reservation 預訂旅館
Transportation 安排交通
Extension 延伸學習

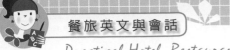

Introduction 學習重點

　　若想要有好的旅遊品質，確保愉快的度假心情，事前的規劃是很重要的。安排旅遊景點、預訂旅館以及安排交通，是本章介紹的重點。

Useful Words 常用字彙

tourist center	遊客中心
public transportation system	大眾交通運輸系統
tourist attraction(=scenic spot)	觀光景點
travel agency	旅行社
map	地圖
historical site	歷史景點
advise	建議／推薦
recommend	建議／推薦
travel magazine	旅遊雜誌

Sightseeing 安排旅遊景點

Useful Expressions 常用的表達方法

1. Would you please tell me some of the attractions here?
   請你告訴我這裡的風景名勝好嗎？
2. Do you know any famous places around here?

你知道這附近有什麼有名的地方嗎？

3. Anything interesting to see in this city?

這座城市有什麼有趣的東西可以看？

4. What would you advise us to see here?

你建議我們在這遊覽什麼地方好？

5. Would you recommend some interesting places to go?

你可以推薦一些有趣的地方嗎？

Are there any _____? 有任何_____嗎？

例句：

1. Are there any scenic spots here？

這裡有什麼觀光景點嗎？

2. Are there any places of historical interest?

這裡有什麼歷史遺跡嗎？

3. Are there any famous mountains and great rivers in the South?

南方有名山大川嗎？

How/what about _____?（提議的時候用）

例句：

1. How about looking around the village by bike?

要不要騎腳踏車遊覽這座村莊呢？

2. What about Niagara Falls?

尼加拉瓜瀑布如何？

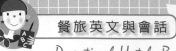

Conversation 會話

(*In a tourist information center*...)

Tourist: I'd like to find more interesting places to visit here.

Receptionist: How about the Central park in this city?

Tourist: That sounds nice. Are there any **guided tours** available there?

Receptionist: Yes, there are. They start every hour and it's for free by the way.

Tourist: How far away is that from here?

Receptionist: It's about ten minutes by taxi.

Tourist: What else would you **advise** us to see?

Receptionist: There are some popular **scenic spots** introduced in this brochure. You can take a look, and there is a map for you, too.

Tourist: Can I take one?

Receptionist: Sure.

（在遊客服務中心。）

遊客：我想在這找更多有趣的地方去看看。

櫃檯人員：要不要去看看市內的中央公園呢？

遊客：聽起來不錯。那邊有導覽嗎？

櫃檯人員：有的。他們每個整點開始解說，而且是免費的。

遊客：那距離這裡多遠？

櫃檯人員：搭計程車大概十分鐘。

遊客：你還建議我們去看什麼？

櫃檯人員：在手冊當中有介紹很多熱門的景點，你可以看一看，那裡
也有地圖可以拿。

遊客：我可以拿一本嗎？

櫃檯人員：當然可以。

Word Bank 重要單字片語

1. guided tour n. phr. 有導遊的遊覽

2. advise [əd`vaɪz] v. 建議

3. scenic [`sɪnɪk] adj. 風景的

4. spot [spɑt] n. 地點

Quiz 小試身手：請寫出正確英文單字

1. 觀光景點：s_____ s_____(= tourist a_____)
2. 有導遊的導覽：g_____ t_____
3. 小冊子：b_____

答案: scenic spot, attraction, guided tour, brochure

Making a Reservation 預訂旅館

Useful Expressions 常用的表達方法

客人

1. Can I reserve a room over the phone, please?
   請問我可以透過電話訂房嗎？

2. I'd like to book/reserve a single room, please.
   我想訂 / 預訂單人房。

3. What's the room rate?
   房間費用怎麼算？

侍者

1. When will you be arriving?
   您何時會抵達？

2. How many nights will you be staying?
   您將會住幾個晚上？

3. How long will you be staying?

您預計住多久？

4. Would you prefer a smoking or non-smoking room?

您偏好吸煙或非吸煙的房間？

5. Would you like a double bed or twin beds?

您想要一張雙人床還是兩張單人床？

6. May I have your name and phone number please?

我可以請問您的大名及電話號碼嗎？

Conversation 會話

(*Booking a room.*)

Receptionist: Vacation Inn. How can I help you?

Guest: Hello, I'd like to reserve a double room for next week.

Receptionist: Certainly, sir. When will you be arriving?

Guest: Well, I'll be arriving on July 18.

Receptionist: And how long will you be staying with us?

Guest: Only one night. I'll be leaving on July 19.

Receptionist: OK. I'll check to see if there are any vacancies. Hold on, please.

Guest:Thank you.

Receptionist: There's no problem, sir. There are rooms available on July 18.

Guest:That's excellent!! Oh, what is the room rate?

Receptionist: It's US$90 plus tax per night for a double room. Would you **prefer** a non-smoking room?

Guest: Yes. Is breakfast included?

Receptionist: Yes, we offer complimentary breakfast.

Guest: OK. Can I reserve a room now?

Receptionist: Of course, sir. May I have your name and telephone number, please?

（預訂房間）

櫃檯人員：假期飯店。我可以為您效勞嗎？

客人：哈囉，我想預訂下週的雙人房。

櫃檯人員：好的，先生。您何時會到達？

客人：嗯，我將會在7月18日到達。

櫃檯人員：您將會住多久？

客人：只有一個晚上。我7月19日會離開。

櫃檯人員：好的，我將為您確認有沒有空房。請稍後。

客人：謝謝你。

櫃檯人員：沒有問題，先生。7月18日有空房。

客人：太棒了！房間的價錢怎麼算？

櫃檯人員：雙人房一晚九十元美金再加稅金。您偏好禁菸的房間嗎？

客人：是的。早餐有包含在內嗎？

櫃檯人員：有的，我們提供免費早餐。

客人：好的，我現在可以訂房了嗎？

櫃檯人員：當然可以，先生。我可以請問您的名字及電話號碼嗎？

Word Bank 重要單字片語

1. prefer [prɪˋfɝ] v. 更喜歡

Quiz 小試身手：請寫出正確英文單字

1. Can I r_____(= book) a room over the phone?

2. What's the room r_____（費用）？ 房間費用怎麼算？

3. Would you p_____（偏好）a smoking or n____s_____ room?

答案：reserve, rate, prefer, non-smoking

Transportation 安排交通

Useful Expressions 常用的表達方法

公車

bus fare	公車票價
bus pass	公車優惠票
bus stop	公車站牌
tour bus	遊覽車

火車

conductor	（火車的）隨車服務員；（電車、巴士的）車掌
dining car	餐車
elevated train	高架鐵路
first class	頭等車廂
monorail	單軌鐵路
platform	月台
railway	鐵路
subway	地下鐵
ticket machine	自動售票機
ticket office	售票處
timetable	時刻表
trolley	電車

船

canoe	獨木舟
life boat	救生艇
ocean liner	遠洋定期客（郵）輪
sailboat	帆船

Conversation 會話

(*A guest is calling to a **travel agency**.*)

Travel agent: Hello. May I help you?

Guest: Yes, I'm planning a trip to London. I'd like to know about the **transportation** system there. How can we travel between two places there?

Travel agent: There is a **railway** system called "the Underground" or "the Tube" by locals. You can travel most of the places by the system.

Guest: Where can I buy the tickets?

Travel agent: There are **staffed** ticket offices, some open for **limited** periods only. Ticket **machines** are **usable** at any time, so you can buy the tickets through the machine.

Guest: Thank you for your help.

（一個客人正打電話到旅行社。）

旅行社職員：哈囉。我可以為您效勞嗎？

客人：是的，我正在計畫去倫敦旅行。我想要知道那邊的交通運輸系統。在那邊我們要怎麼往返兩地？

旅行社職員：那裡有鐵路系統，被當地人稱為 "the Underground" 或是" the Tube "。您可以藉由這個系統遊覽大部分的地方。

客人：我可以在哪裡買票？

旅行社職員：那邊有配有職員的售票口，有些只開放有限的時段。售票機任何時候都可以用，所以您可以透過售票機買票。

客人：謝謝你的幫忙。

Word Bank 重要單字片語

1. travel agency n. phr. 旅行社

2. travel agent n. phr. 旅行社職員

3. transportation [ˌtrænspɔrˋteʃən] n. 運輸

4. railway [ˋrelˌwe] n. 鐵路；鐵道

5. local [ˋlokl̩] n. 當地居民；本地人

6. staff [stæf] v. 給…配備職員

7. limited [ˋlɪmɪtɪd] n. 有限的

8. machine [məˋʃɪn] n. 機器

9. usable [ˋjuzəbl̩] adj. 可用的

Quiz 小試身手：請寫出正確英文單字

1. 售票機：t_____ m_____

2. 旅行社 / 旅行社職員：t_____ a_____/a_____

3. 運輸：t_____

答案：ticket machine, travel agency/agent, transportation

Extension 延伸學習：B&B民宿

在台灣民宿的分布越來越普遍，『民宿』的英文怎麼說？

B&B (Bed+Breakfast)：

民宿還可分為家庭式、旅館式、度假別墅、飯店等。

1. Homestay B&B

2. B&B Inns

3. B&B Cottages

4. B&B Hotels

5. guest house（寄宿的概念）

民宿的住宿資訊：房間特色

‧ Ocean View Suite 海景套房

‧ Maximum Occupancy: 2 最多可容納二人

‧ Air-conditioned 空調

‧ Windows(can see the best ocean view) 窗戶（可看見最佳海景）

‧ Sofa, in room 房內有沙發

‧ TV features: remote control, LCD TV 47 inch

　47吋液晶電視、遙控器

‧ Cable channels include CNN, NHK and ESPN

　有線電視頻道包括CNN, NHK, HBO, ESPN

‧ High speed uireless internet, for free 免費高速無線網路

‧ Bicycles available 提供腳踏車

‧ Charge:US80$ 實用：美金80元

‧ Check in 2:30pm 入住：下午二點半

‧ Check out 11:30am 退房：上午十一點半

單一選擇題 Multiple Choice

1. We wanted to book a hotel room in April but there were no _____

   (A) attractions (B) locals (C) vacancies (D) tourists

2. Can you _____ where we might visit?

   (A) ask (B) tell (C) doubt (D) suggest.

3. The bread is popular with both visitors and _____.

   (A) railways (B) spots (C) machines (D) locals

4. This looks like a great _____ for a visit.

   (A) spot (B) plane (C) vacancy (D) canoe.

5. I'd like to go there by using _____system.

   (A) phone (B) platform (C) transportation (D) hotel

6. Millions of _____ visit Disneyworld each year.

   (A) spots (B) tourists (C) tickets (D) schedules

7. Life in Paris has so many _____ - department stores, good restaurants and so on.

   (A) people (B) plans (C) attractions (D) agents

8. London is the capital _____ of England.

   (A) country (B) city (C) land (D) location

9. I help Laura to _____her route during this summer vacation.

   (A) plan (B) page (C) store (D) pick

10. There are many nice scenic spots introduced in this _____.

    (A) brochure (B) visit (C) stay (D) plan

11. Jane: _____

    Receptionist: How about National Palace Museum?

    (A) What would you recommend for dinner?

    (B) Would you please tell me some of scenic spots here?

    (C) How's the weather?

    (D) How many of you in your party?

12. Jane: How can we travel between Taipei and Kaohsiung?

    Receptionist: _____.

    (A) By credit card.

    (B) Either by bus or train.

    (C) It's about four hours.

    (D) It's more than 100 kilometers.

13. Receptionist: Vacation Hotel. How can I help you?

    Jane: Good afternoon, _____

    Receptionist: I'll check for you, sir.

    (A) there are no rooms available.

    (B) I would like to settle the bill.

    (C) there is a single room.

    (D) I'd like to reserve a double room for next Friday.

14. Receptionist: How about Yangmingshan National Park?

    Tourist: _____

Receptionist: There are some popular scenic spots such as Danshuei, Shida night market, or Lungshan Temple.

(A) What else would you recommend?

(B) Where can I take the bus?

(C) Where would you like to see?

(D) What's your favorite food?

15. Receptionist: How long will you be staying with us?

Guest: Only one night. _____.

Receptionist: OK. I'll check to see if there are any vacancies.

(A) Next week.

(B) I'll get there by taxi.

(C) I'll arrive in your hotel at 2 pm.

(D) I'll be leaving on May 19th.

答案：(C)(D)(D)(A)(C)(B)(C)(B)(A)(A)
　　　(B)(B)(D)(A)(D)

In the Airport

14 航空

 本章摘要

Booking a Ticket 預訂機位
Confirming a Reservation 確認班機
Check-in 登機手續
Check-in Baggage/Forwards Luggage 行李託運
A Security Check 安檢通關
Missing Luggage 行李遺失
Extension 延伸學習

Introduction 學習重點

　　航空是本書最後一章，也是最後一個大重點。包括預訂機位、確認班機、登機手續、行李託運、安檢通關以及行李遺失，本章將逐一介紹。

Useful Words 常用字彙

機場大廳

airport	機場
airport tax	機場稅
arrival	到達
cart	推車
check-in counter	辦理登機手續的櫃檯
departure	離境
duty-free shop	免稅商店
gate	登機門
ground crew	地勤人員
lost and found	失物招領處
lounge area	候機室
luggage carousel	行李的旋轉運輸帶
shuttle bus	往返機場的接駁巴士
terminal	機場大廈／航站
transit	過境

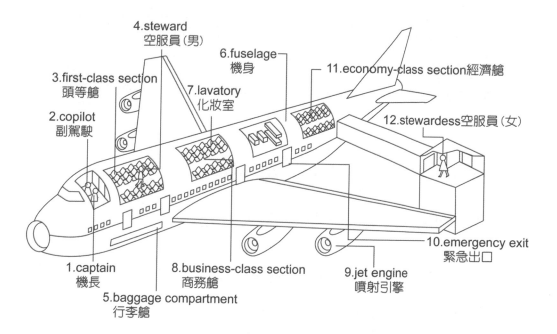

4.steward
空服員(男)

6.fuselage
機身

11.economy-class section經濟艙

3.first-class section
頭等艙

7.lavatory
化妝室

2.copilot
副駕駛

12.stewardess空服員(女)

1.captain
機長

8.business-class section
商務艙

9.jet engine
噴射引擎

10.emergency exit
緊急出口

5.baggage compartment
行李艙

在飛機上

aisle	走道
aisle seat	走道座位
window seat	靠窗座位
middle seat	中間座位
overhead compartment	座位上方行李廂
oxygen mask	氧氣罩
seat belt	安全帶
armrest	扶手
foldaway table	摺疊式餐桌
galley	飛機上的廚房

airsickness bag	嘔吐袋
headphones	頭戴式耳機
in-flight music/sales/movie	機內音樂／機上免稅販賣／電影

Booking a Ticket 預訂機位

Useful Expressions 常用的表達方法

訂票櫃檯人員

1. What's your destination and travel date?

   請問您的目的地及旅程時間？

2. Which class do you prefer, economy class, business class, or the first class?

   您偏好那個座艙，經濟艙、商務艙還是頭等艙？

3. One-way ticket or round-trip ticket?

   單程票還是來回票？

Conversation 會話

(*A caller is booking a ticket.*)

Reservation officer: Hello! How can I help you?

Caller: I'd like to book a ticket.

Reservation officer: What's your **destination** and travel date, sir?

Caller: I'll be leaving on March 2nd to New York.

Reservation officer: Which class do you prefer, economy class, business class, or the first class?

Caller: Economy class.

Reservation officer: One-way ticket or round-trip ticket, sir?

Caller: Round trip.

Reservation officer: OK. You'd like to book a round trip ticket to New York for March 2nd. Booking class is Economy class. Is that correct?

Caller: Yes. By the way, I don't want a night flight, please.

Reservation officer: OK. May I have your English name and your contact phone number, please?

Caller: My name is John Robinson. My mobile phone number is 0900-007-007.

Reservation officer: Thank you. You will take the 10:30 CAL Flight 238 on March 2nd. Have a nice day.

（客人來電訂機票。）

訂票櫃檯人員：哈囉。我可以為您效勞嗎？

來電者：我想要訂票。

訂票櫃檯人員：先生，請問您的目的地及旅程時間？

來電者：我預計3月2日要到紐約。

訂票櫃檯人員：您要坐那個座艙，經濟艙、商務艙、還是頭等艙？

來電者：經濟艙。

訂票櫃檯人員：單程票還是來回票，先生？

來電者：來回票。

訂票櫃檯人員：好的，您訂了3月2日到紐約的來回票。預定的座艙是經濟艙。對嗎？

來電者：是的。對了，請不要幫我安排晚上的班機。

訂票櫃檯人員：好的，我可以請問您的英文名字以及聯絡電話嗎？

來電者：我的名字是約翰・羅賓森。手機號碼是0900-007-007。

訂票櫃檯人員：謝謝你。您的班機是3月2日十點半華航238班機。祝您有個愉快的一天。

Word Bank 重要單字片語

1. destination [ˌdɛstəˋneʃən] n. 目的地；終點

Quiz 小試身手：請寫出正確英文單字

Passenger: May I have an a_____ s_____（靠走道的位置）

　　　　　please?

Check-in Assistant: If you'll wait a minute, I'll find out for you.

(*After about one minute...*)

Check-in Assistant: Sorry, sir. We don't have window seats

　　　　　a_____（可被使用的）on this f_____

　　　　　（班機）.

Passenger: That's OK.

答案：1. aisle 2. seat 3. available 4. flight

Confirming a Reservation 確認班機

Useful Expressions 常用的表達方法

訂票櫃檯人員

1. Does your schedule remain unchanged?

　　您的行程保持不變嗎？

2. May I have your name and contact phone?

　　可以請問您的名字及連絡電話嗎？

3. We will appreciate it very much if you would notify us of your

　　cancellation.

　　如果您可以先通知我們您要取消，我們會非常感激。

Conversation 會話

(*A caller is calling to confirm his plane reservation.*)

Reservation officer: Reservation office. May I help you?

Caller: Yes, I'd like to **reconfirm** my plane reservation.

Reservation officer: Does your schedule remain unchanged?

Caller: Yes.

Reservation officer: May I have your name and contact phone, please?

Caller: My name is John Robinson. My phone number is 0900-007-007.

Reservation officer: You've booked a round trip ticket to New York on March 2nd.

Caller: Thank you. If I need to make some changes on the ticket, what should I do?

Reservation officer: We will appreciate it very much if you would **notify** us of your **cancellation**. In this way, other passengers on the waiting list can be **accommodated**.

Caller: I see.

Reservation officer: Please remember you'll have to get to the airport three hours before the take-off time.

（有人打電話來確認預定的機票。）

訂票櫃檯人員：訂票櫃檯。我可以為您效勞嗎？

來電者：是的，我想確認我預訂的機票。

訂票櫃檯人員：您的行程保持不變嗎？

來電者：是的。

訂票櫃檯人員：可以請問您的名字及連絡電話嗎？

來電者：我的名字是約翰‧羅賓森，手機號碼是0900-007-007.

訂票櫃檯人員：您訂了3月2日到紐約的來回票。

來電者：謝謝你。如果我的機票需要變更，我該怎麼做？

訂票櫃檯人員：不客氣。如果您可以先通知我們您要取消，我們會非常感激。如此一來，其他在等待的乘客就能搭上飛機。

來電者：我知道了。

訂票櫃檯人員：請記得您必須在起飛三個小時前到達機場。

Word Bank 重要單字片語

1. reconfirm [ˌrɪkənˋfɝm] v. 再證實；再確認；再確定

2. notify [ˋnotəˌfaɪ] v. 通知；告知

3. cancellation [ˌkænsḷˋeʃən] n. 取消

4. accommodate [əˋkɑməˌdet] v. 能容納；（飛機等）可搭載

Quiz 小試身手：請寫出正確英文單字

officer: R_____（預訂機位）office. How can I help you?

Caller: Yes, I'd like to r_____m（再確認）my plane reservation.

officer: Does your s_____（行程）remain un_____（不變）?

Caller: Yes.

答案：Reservation, reconfirm, schedule, unchanged

Check-in 登機手續

Useful Expressions 常用的表達方法

證件

1. Can I see your ticket, please?

   請問我可以看您的機票嗎？

2. May I have your passport, please?

   請問我可以看您的護照嗎？

3. Do you have your passport with you?

   您有帶護照嗎？

4. I'm afraid your passport has expired.

   恐怕您的護照已經過期了。

5. Do you have a second piece of identification?

   您有第二身分證件嗎？

6. I'll need to see your child's birth certificate.

我需要看您小孩的出生證明。

旅客需求

1. Would you like an aisle or a window seat?

您想要走道或是靠窗的位置？

2. Would you like a wheelchair?

您要輪椅嗎？

3. Did you request a vegetarian meal?

您有要求素食餐嗎？

登機門

1. You'll board at Gate 4.

您將在四號登機門登機。

2. Please be at the gate thirty minutes before your scheduled flight.

請在您飛機預計起飛的三十分鐘前到登機門。

班機訊息

1. Your flight is expected to take off on time.

您的班機預計會準時起飛。

2. Your flight has been delayed by one hour.

您的班機已經延誤一個小時了。

3. Flight XXX to_____ (Tokyo, Taipei) has been canceled.

XXX到_____（東京、台北）的班機已經停飛。

其他

1. I'm afraid that you're too late to check-in.

恐怕您太晚來辦登機手續了。

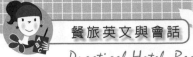
2. Your flight is overbooked. Would you be interested in giving up your seat?

您的班機已經超額訂位了。您有興趣放棄您的機位嗎？

3. Enjoy your flight.

祝您搭機愉快。

Conversation 會話

(*A passenger is checking in.*)

Passenger: Is this the CAL Airlines check-in?

Check-in Assistant: Yes. May I help you?

Passenger: Yes. Here are my ticket and passport. I'm going to Tokyo. I want to check these two pieces. Are they **overweight**?

Check-in Assistant: No. They weigh fifteen kilos. They'll be just under the weight. Are you keeping that small bag as **hand-luggage**?

Passenger: Yes, I'll carry this bag by myself. May I have a window seat please?

Check-in Assistant: If you'll wait a minute, I'll find out for you.

(*After about one minute...*)

Check-in Assistant: I'm sorry, sir. We don't have window seats available on this flight.

Passenger: That's OK.

Check-in Assistant: Here you go, sir. This is your **boarding pass**. Be at the Gate 5 one hour prior to boarding time. Have a nice day.

Passenger: Thank you.

（乘客正在辦登機手續。）

乘客：這是華航的登機櫃檯嗎？

登機櫃檯人員：是的。我可以為您效勞嗎？

乘客：這是我的機票和護照。我要去東京。我想要託運這兩件行李。有超重嗎？

登機櫃檯人員：沒有。它們重十五公斤。剛好沒超過重量限制。您要攜帶這個小包包當隨身行李嗎？

乘客：是的，這個包包我會自己帶。請給我靠窗的位置好嗎？

登機櫃檯人員：請等我幾分鐘，我幫您找一下。

（過了大約一分鐘…）

登機櫃檯人員：我很抱歉，先生。這個班機沒有空的靠窗位置了。

乘客：沒關係。

登機櫃檯人員：先生，給您。這是您的登機證。請在登機時間一小時前到達5號登機門。祝您有愉快的一天。

乘客：謝謝你。

Word Bank 重要單字片語

1. overweight [`ovɚ`we] adj. 超重的；過重的

2. hand-luggage n. 手提行李；隨身行李

3. boarding pass [`bɔrdɪŋˌpæs] n. phr. 登機證

Quiz 小試身手：請寫出正確英文單字

1. 素食餐：v_____ m_____

2. 過期: e_____

3. 身分證明：i_____

4. 手提行李：h_____-l_____

5. 登機證: b_____ p_____

答案：vegetarian meal, expire, identification, hand-luggage, boarding pass

Check-in Baggage/Forwards Luggage
行李託運

Useful Expressions 常用的表達方法

1. How many bags are you checking?

   您有多少行李要拖運？

2. Will you be bringing a carry-on bag?

   您有隨身包包嗎？

3. Do you have any hand / hand-carried luggage?

   您有任何隨身行李嗎？

行李是否過重

1. I'm afraid that bag exceeds the size restriction.

   恐怕行李超過大小限制。

2. I'm afraid there'll be an excess baggage charge.

恐怕會有額外的行李費用。

3. It's _____(e.g. ten) kilos overweight.

超重 _____ （例：十公斤）

4. It's _____(e.g. two) pounds over.

超過_____ （例：二磅）。

5. The free allowance for luggage is _____(e.g. twenty kilos).

免費的行李重量限額是_____ （例：二十公斤）。

6. There's no excess to pay.

沒有超重費用要付。

行李標籤

1. Did you need any tags for your luggage?

您需要行李標籤嗎？

2. Is your luggage properly labeled?

您的行李適當用籤條標明了嗎？

Conversation 會話

（*Forwarding luggage*）

Check-in Assistant: May I have your passport and ticket, please?

How many **pieces** of luggage do you want to check, ma'am?

Passenger: I've got three pieces altogether.

Check-in Assistant: Would you put your luggage on the **counter**?

Passenger: OK. Are they overweight?

Check-in Assistant: You're allowed only 25 pounds of luggage. You've got 7 kilos of **excess** baggage.

Passenger: Oh, do I need to pay for the excess luggage?

Check-in Assistant: Yes, or you may take one of them as **carry-on** baggage.

Passenger: OK, I'll take this one. Thank you.

Check-in Assistant: Could you put on the luggage **label**, please.

Passenger: Sure.

（托運行李）

報到櫃檯人員：可以給我看您的機票及護照嗎？您有多少行李要託運，女士？

乘客：總共有三件。

報到櫃檯人員：可以請您將行李放在櫃檯上嗎？

乘客：好的。有超重嗎？

報到櫃檯人員：您行李重量的限額是二十五磅。您的行李超重七公斤。

乘客：我需要付超重費用嗎？

報到櫃檯人員：是的，或是您可能可以拿其中一個當作隨身行李。

乘客：好的，我拿這個。謝謝你。

報到櫃檯人員：可以請貼上行李標籤，好嗎？

乘客：好的。

Word Bank 重要單字片語

1. piece [pis] n. 一件

2. counter [ˈkɑʊntɚ] n. 櫃臺

3. excess [ɪkˈsɛs] n. 超額量

4. carry-on [ˈkærɪɑn] adj. 隨身攜帶的

5. label [ˈlebl̩] n. 貼紙；標籤

Quiz 小試身手：請寫出正確英文單字

1. I'm afraid that bag exceeds the size r_____（限制）.

2. Could you put on the luggage l_____（標籤）?

3. I'm afraid there'll be an e_____（額外的） baggage charge.

4. How many p_____（件）of luggage do you want to check, ma'am?

答案：restriction , label(s) , excess , pieces

A Security Check 安檢通關

Useful Expressions 常用的表達方法

安全檢查人員

1. Please put all your baggage on the scanner and take off your shoes.

   請把行李放在這個掃描器上,然後脫掉您的鞋子。

2. If you have any metal objects, please put them on plastic tray at the side.

   如果您有金屬的物件,請放在那邊的托盤上。

3. Raise your arms and stand still.

   舉起手臂,並站直。

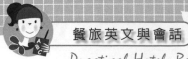
Conversation 會話

(*A security officer is checking baggage*...)

Security officer: Please put all your baggage on the machine and take off your shoes.

Passenger: OK.

(*The passenger puts all his baggage on the **scanner** and takes off his shoes*.)

Security officer: If you have any **metal** objects, such as keys or coins, please put them in the plastic tray at the side.

Passenger: I didn't bring any metal.

Security officer: OK. This way, please. Now, pass through the scanner.

(*The guest passes through the scanner*.)

Security officer: Please raise your arms and stand **still**.

(*The security officer checks the passenger's clothes and **pockets**.*)

Security officer: OK. Thanks for your **cooperation**. Now you can take back your bags.

（安全檢查人員正在檢查行李⋯）
安全檢查人員：請把行李放在這個機器上，然後脫掉您的鞋子。

乘客：好的

（乘客把行李放在這個掃描器上，並脫掉他的鞋子。）

安全檢查人員：如果您有金屬的物件，像鑰匙或是硬幣，請放在那邊
　　　　　　　　的托盤上。

乘客：我沒有帶任何金屬。

安全檢查人員：好的。這邊請。請通過掃描器。

（乘客通過掃描器。）

安全檢查人員：請舉起手臂，並站直。

（安檢人員檢查乘客的衣服與口袋。）

安全檢查人員：好的，謝謝您的合作。現在您可以拿回您的行李。

Word Bank 重要單字片語

1. scanner [ˋskænɚ] n. 掃描機

2. metal [ˋmɛtl̩] n. 金屬

3. plastic [ˋplæstɪk] adj. 塑膠的

4. still [stɪl] adj. 靜止的；不動的

5. pocket [ˋpɑkɪt] n. 口袋

6. cooperation [koˏɑpəˋreʃən] n. 合作

Quiz 小試身手：請寫出正確英文單字

1. Please r_____（舉起）your arms and stand s_____（靜止不
   動）.

2. Please put all your baggage on the m_____e（機器）and
   _____ _____（脫掉）your shoes.

3. Now, pass through the s_____r（掃描器）.

答案：1. raise, still 2. machine, take off 3. scanner

大哉問：到達當地，要入境過海關時會遇到哪些問題？

the interview with immigration

1. How long will you stay?
   你預計停留多久

2. What's your purpose of this trip？
   來美國的目的

3. Where are you going to stay？
   你預計在那裡停留

4. Do you have any family members or friends traveling with you?
   有同行的親戚朋友嗎？

Missing Luggage 行李遺失

Useful Expressions 常用的表達方法

行李遺失部門

1. I'll tell the baggage handlers to look for it.
   我將會告訴搬運行李的人去尋找。

2. Please give me your contact number and the address of the hotel you'll be staying.
   請給我您的聯絡電話，以及您將住宿的飯店地址。

3. We'll contact you and forward it there right after we find your luggage.
   一找到您的行李之後，我們將會連絡您，且送過去。

Conversation 會話

(*A passenger's luggage is missing.*)

Passenger: My luggage is not here. Here are my luggage tags.

Lost luggage Department： Please tell me the flight you took.

Passenger: Flight 288 from New York.

Lost luggage Department： OK. I'll tell the baggage **handlers** to look for it.

Passenger: I can't wait for too long. I have a meeting after half an hour.

Lost luggage Department： Please give me your contact number and the address of the hotel you'll be staying at. We'll contact you and **forward** it there right after we find your luggage.

Passenger: I'll be staying at Room 808 in the Hilton Hotel. Please try to send my luggage back later tonight.

Lost luggage Department: We'll try our best. You can call this **toll-free** number to ask me if you have any problems. My name is Jessie.

Passenger: Thank you.

（乘客的行李不見了。）

乘客：我的行李不在這裡。這是我的行李標籤。

行李遺失部門：請告訴我您所搭的班機。

乘客：紐約出發的288班機。

行李遺失部門：好的。我會告知搬運行李的人去尋找。

乘客：我無法等太久。我半個小時後有一個會議。

行李遺失部門：請給我您的聯絡電話，以及您將住宿的飯店地址，一找到您的行李之後，我們將會連絡您，且送過去。

乘客：我會住在希爾頓飯店808號房。請盡量在今晚將我的行李送回。

行李遺失部門：我們會盡力。如果您有任何問題的話，您可以打這個免付費號碼來問我。我的名字是潔西。

乘客：謝謝你。

Word Bank 重要單字片語

1. handler [`hændl̩] n. 搬運者

2. forward [`fɔrwɚd] v. 發送；轉交

3. toll-free [ˌto`fri] adj. 不用付電話費的

Quiz 小試身手：請寫出正確英文單字

1. 搬運行李的人：b_____ h_____

2. 行李標籤：l_____ t____

3. 發送；轉交：f_____d

答案：baddage handler, luggage tag, forward

Extension 延伸學習：其他相關資訊

入出境卡、海關申報表

飛機即將抵達目的地時，旅客必須填寫的表格。

出入境卡

包括班機資訊、護照號碼、國籍、姓名等等。

Arrival/ Departure Card

1. flight number _____

2. pass port number _____

3. nationality as shown on passport _____

4. family name _____

5. given or first name _____

6. date of birth day _____ month _____ year _____

7. occupation or job _____

8. full contact or residential address

_____

9. overseas port where you boarded this aircraft

_____

海關申報表

針對旅客所攜帶的行李所填寫的申報表。

Customs Declaration Form

1. Family name _____

   Given _____ Middle _____

2. Birthdate Day _____ Month _____ Year _____

3. Hotel name/ Destination

_____

4. Passport issued by (country) _____

5. Passport number _____

6. Airline/flight number _____

7. The primary purpose of this trip is business Yes_____

   No_____

8. I am (We are) bringing

(a) fruits, vegetables, plants, seeds, food, insects Yes_____

   No_____

(b) meats, animals, animal/wildlife products Yes_____ No_____

(c) disease agents, cell cultures, snails Yes_____ No_____

(d) soil or have been on a farm/ranch/ pasture

9. I have (We have) been in close proximity of (such as touching

   or handling) live stock Yes_____ No_____

10. I am carrying currency or monetary instrument over

   Yes_____ No_____

機場詞彙對照表

Domestic Terminal	國內線航站
International Terminal	國際線航站
Cargo Terminal	貨運站
Maintenance Hanger	維修棚廠
One-way ticket	單程票
Round-trip ticket	來回票
Carry-on Bag	手提行李
Bonded Baggage	存關行李
Luggage Tag	行李標籤
Luggage Cart(Trolley)	行李手推車
Baggage Baling Service	行李打包服務
Information Counter	服務台
Customs Service Counter	海關服務櫃檯
Immigration Office	入出境辦公室
Animal & Plant Quarantine	動植物檢疫局
Tourism Bureau Service Center	觀光局旅客服務中心
Association of Travel Agents Information	旅行同業公會服務櫃檯
National Museum of History	國立歷史博物館
Change planes	轉機
Non-stop(direct)flight	直達航班

Coin Locker	投幣式寄物櫃
Smoking Room	吸煙室
Praying Room	祈禱室
Foreign Currency Exchange	外幣兌換
Restaurant	餐廳
Duty-Free Shop	免稅商店
Rental Counter	租車櫃檯
Insurance Counter	保險
Public Telephone	公共電話
ATM	自動提款機
Service For The Disabled	身心障礙服務
Runway	跑道
Apron	停機坪
Ramp	空橋
Greeting Area	到站等候區
Control Tower	塔台
Remove Parking Bay	接駁停機坪
Departure	出境
Arrival	入境
Arirlines	航空公司
Mandarin Aivlines	華信航空
UNI AIR	立榮航空

Far Eastern Air Transport	遠東航空
Tran Asia Airways	復興航空
China Airlines	中華航空
EVA AIR	長榮航空
DRAGONAIR	港龍航空
Japan Asia Airways	日本亞細亞航空
Thai Airlines	泰國航空
Malaysia Airlines	馬來西亞航空
Pacific Airlines	越南太平洋航空
Viet Air	越南航空
Air Macau	澳門航空
Cathay Pacific Airways	國泰航空
SINGAPORE AIRLINES	新加坡航空
UNITED AIRLINES	聯合航空
NORTHWEST AIRLINES	西北航空
KOREAN AIR	大韓航空
Asiana	韓亞航空
All Nippon Airways	日空航空
Philippine Airlines	菲律賓航空
Garuda Indonesia	印尼航空
KLM Royal Dutch Airlines	荷蘭航空
President Airlines	柬埔寨總統航空

Luggage Scale	行李磅秤
Waiting Room	候機室
Flight Information Board	航班顯示看板
On Time	準時
Delay	延誤
Timetable	時刻表
VIP Lounges	貴賓室
Shuttle Bus	接駁車
Transit Room	過境室
Arrival Lobby	入境大廳
Baggage Delivery	行李托運
Baggage Claim	提領行李
Stand-by	候補機位

資料來源：台灣桃園國際機場網站；作者整理

Multiple Choice 單一選擇題

1. _____ 515 to New York is now boarding at gate 6.

   (A) Schedule (B) Class (C) Flight (D) Label

2. We expect to be landing at Paris in an hour's time according to _____ speaking.

   (A) captain's (B) teacher's (C) president's (D) officer's

3. Remember to put an address _____ on the luggage.

   (A) label (B) flight (C) level (D) pass

4. We always fly _____ class because of lacking money.

   (A) history (B) economy (C) business (D) first

5. Our _____ was delayed because we were in bad weather.

   (A) compartment (B) ticket (C) gate (D) departure.

6. I have to check your _____ and ticket before you board.

   (A) tag (B) passport (C) piece (D) purpose

7. All the plane tickets were sold out, so we waited to see if there were any _____.

   (A) attendants (B) captains (C) cancellations (D) rooms

8. Passengers for flight LK158 please go to _____ 9.

   (A) economy class (B) passport (C) gate (D) ticket

9. You might read the bus _____ before you go out.

   (A) schedule (B) arrival (C) vacancy (D) system

10. The plane will _____ at 7.30 p.m.

(A) turn off (B) make up (C) clean up (D) take off

11. Please bring your _____ pass to gate 10.

(A) ticket (B) broad (C) luggage (D) boarding.

12. If you have any _____ objects, put them on the plastic tray.

(A) local (B) expensive (C) metal (D) wood

13. All _____ luggage must be stored under your seat.

(A) pocket (B) carry-on (C) scanner (D) immigration

14. We can buy something _____ when we're waiting at the airport.

(A) duty-free (B) expensive (C) still (D) free

15. You need to pay for your _____ luggage.

(A) excess (B) exit (C) cooperation (D) departure

16. Wait me for a while. I will go to the luggage _____ area for my bag.

(A) arrival (B) custom (C) claim (D) immigration

17. A: How _____ will you stay here?

B: Six days.

(A) long (B) often (C) far (D) much

18. Officer: May I have your passport, please?

Jane: _____

(A) Yes, they are.

(B) I have no idea.

(C) Here you are.

(D) Here is the hotel.

19. Officer: _____

Jane: I am here to do some sight-seeing.

(A) How long will you stay here?

(B) Where are you going to stay?

(C) Where are you from?

(D) What's the purpose of your visit?

20. Check-in Assistant: Good morning, sir. May I help you?

Passenger: Yes. I'm going to Tokyo. I want to check these three pieces. _____

Check-in Assistant: No. They'll be just under the weight.

(A) How much is it?

(B) Are they overweight?

(C) Here are my ticket and passport.

(D) When will they arrive?

21. Reservation officer: You'd like to book a round trip ticket to Tokyo for July 2nd. _____ Is that correct?

Caller: Yes.

(A) Pass through the scanner.

(B) Booking class is Business Class.

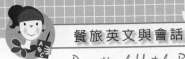

(C) Flight 259 to New York.

(D) The excess charge will be NT $ 200.

22. Reservation officer: _____, economy class,

business class, or first class?

Caller: Economy class.

(A) Which class do you prefer

(B) What would you recommend

(C) Which flight would you like to take

(D) How many bags are you checking

23. Reservation officer: _____Do you have a

second piece of identification?

Passenger: Yes, it's my student ID card.

(A) I'm sorry for the delay.

(B) What's your destination and travel date, sir?

(C) I'm afraid your passport has expired.

(D) Please raise your arms and stand still.

24. Check-in Assistant: _____

Passenger: Yes, I'll carry this bag by myself.

(A) Are you keeping the blue bag as hand-luggage?

(B) Thanks for your cooperation.

(C) Do I need to pay for the excess luggage?

(D) May I have your passport, please?

25. Passenger: My luggage is not here.

    Lost luggage Department: _____ I'll tell the

    baggage handlers to look for it.

    (A) Would you please do me a favor?

    (B) Please give me your luggage tags.

    (C) Please give me a brief description of your daughter.

    (D) Excuse me.

26. Security officer: Please raise your arms and stand still.

    What is the security officer going to do?（請選出一個適當的描述。）

    (A) He is going to pass through the scanner.

    (B) He is going to take off his shoes.

    (C) He is going to check the passenger's clothes and pockets.

    (D) He is going to put all his baggage on the scanner.

27. Security officer: This way, please. Please pass through the scanner.

    (*The guest passes through the scanner.*)

    Security officer: OK._____.

    (A) Please give me your luggage tags.

    (B) There's no excess to pay.

    (C) Thanks for your cooperation

    (D) Would you like an aisle or a window seat?

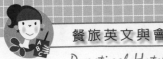
28. Check-in Assistant: How many pieces of luggage do you want to check, sir?

   Passenger: I've got two pieces altogether.

   Check-in Assistant: _____

   (A) May I have a window seat?

   (B) Could you put on the luggage label, please.

   (C) Are they overweight?

   (D) Which class do you prefer?

29. Passenger: Do I need to pay for the excess luggage?

   Check-in Assistant: Yes, _____

   （選錯的）

   (A) I'm afraid there'll be an excess baggage charge.

   (B) or you may take one of them as carry-on baggage.

   (C) it's NT $ 120 dollars.

   (D) There's no excess to pay.

30. Check-in Assistant: Here you go, ma'am. _____ Please be at the Gate 6 thirty minutes prior to the boarding time.

   Passenger: Thank you.

   (A) That's my fault.

   (B) This is your boarding pass.

   (C) This is your luggage tag.

   (D) It's my pleasure.

答案：(C)(A)(A)(B)(D)(B)(C)(C)(A)(D)

(D)(C)(B)(A)(A)(C)(A)(C)(D)(B)

(B)(A)(C)(A)(B)(C)(C)(B)(D)(B)

附錄：重要單字片語整理表

A

accidentally adv. 偶然地；意外地

accommodate v. 能容納；（飛機等）可搭載

accommodation n. 住處；膳宿

accompany v. 陪同；伴隨

add v. 添加；增加

additionally adv. 附加地；同時；此外

address n. 住址；地址

adjust v. 調整

adult n. 成年人

advise v. 建議

airmail n. 航空郵件

airport n. 機場

along with 與…在一起；在…以外

amenity n. 便利設施（常用複數形式）

American-style breakfast n. phr. 美式早餐

appointment n.（尤指正式的）約會

appreciate v. 感謝；感激

arrival n. 到達

as soon as possible 盡快

ask v. 要求；詢問

at once 馬上；立刻

available adj. 可用的；有空的

B

beer n. 啤酒

bellhop n. 行李員

belongings n. 財產；攜帶物品

bill n. [美]鈔票

boarding pass n. phr. 登機證

boutique n. 精品店

breakfast voucher n. phr. 早餐券

brief adj. 簡略的；簡短的

bring v. 帶來；拿來（bring-brought-brought）

broadcast n. 播放

buffet n. 自助餐

built （build的過去分詞 v. 建造）

by the way 順便一提

C

cab n. 計程車

cable n. 有線電視

cancellation n. 取消

carelessness n. 粗心大意

carry-on adj. 隨身攜帶的

cash n. 現金

certainly adv.（用於回答）當然；可以；沒問題

change n. 零錢

charge n. 費用

chart n. 圖表

check v. 檢查；檢驗；核對

children n. 小孩（單數為child）

choice n. 選擇

claim n. 所有權；索回

climate n. 氣候

closed（close的過去分詞 v. 關閉）

clutch bag n. 女用無帶提包

come to v. phr. 共計…

company n. 公司

complementary breakfast 免費早餐

complete adj. 完整的；全部的

connect v. 給…接通電話[(+with)]

contact v. 聯絡

convenience n. 方便；合宜

convert v. 轉換

cooperation n. 合作

correct adj. 正確的

cost n. 費用

counter n. 櫃臺

cube n. 立方體（在此為冰塊）

currency n. 貨幣

D

deduct v. 扣除；減除

deliver v. 投遞；傳送；運送

denomination n.（貨幣等的）面額

department n.（企業等的）部門

deposit n. 保證金；押金；訂金

deposit v. 放置；寄存

describe v. 描述

description n. 描寫；敘述

destination n. 目的地；終點

develop v. 使成長；使發達；發展

dial v. 撥號；打電話

diamond n. 鑽石

difference n. 差距；差額

digit n. 數字

direct v.給…指路

Disneyland n. 迪士尼樂園

dispatch n. 派遣；發送

double check v.phr. 仔細的檢查

drawer n. 抽屜

dressing n.（拌沙拉等用的）調料

dressing table n. phr. 梳妝臺；鏡臺

dry-clean v. 乾洗（衣物）

E

earrings n. 耳環

edit v. 編輯；校訂

effort n.[U][C] 努力；盡力

exceed v. 超出

excess n. 超額量

exchange v. 交換；兌換

exchange rate n. phr. 外匯率

Excuse me. 不好意思（通常是有所請求時說）

expect v. 期待；等待；盼望

expiration date n. phr. 到期日；截止期

extra adj. 額外的；另外收費的

F

favor v. 恩惠

fill out (the form) v. phr. 填寫（表格）

finish v. 用完；吃完

fix v. 修理

forecast n. 預報；預測

forward v. 發送；轉交

frequently adv. 頻繁地；屢次地

full adj. 完全的；完整的

full sized 大型的

G

gather v. 集合

get a cold v. phr. 感冒

get off v. phr 下車

get sth. out of one's way 把sth.移開某人的視線範圍

gratitude n.感激之情；感恩；感謝

group n. 群；團體

guided tour n. phr. 有導遊的遊覽

H

half adj. 一半；二分之一

handler n. 搬運者

hand-luggage 手提行李

harbor n. 港灣；海港

help oneself v. phr. 自行取用

hold v. 舉行（hold-held-held）

Hold on a minute, please. 請稍帶片刻

honor v. 承兌；支付

however adv. 然而

I

ice cube n. phr. 冰塊

immediately adv. 立即；即刻

in a hurry 匆匆；趕時間

include v. 包括；包含

inconvenience n.不便

industry n. 工業；企業；行業

inform v. 通知；告知；報告

information desk n. phr. 詢問處；服務台

international adj. 國際性的；國際間的

intersection n. 道路交叉口；十字路口

invoice n. 發票；發貨單

invoice number n. phr. 統一編號

island n. 島

It's very kind of you. 你人真好

J

just in case 以防萬一

K

king sized 超過標準長度的；加大的

L

label n. 貼紙；標籤

laundry n. 送洗的衣服

leather n. 皮革製品

leave v. 離開（leave-left-left）

limited n. 有限的

local n. 當地居民；本地人

look forward to v. phr. 期待

lotion n. 乳液

luggage n. [U] 行李

M

machine n. 機器

Maokong Gondola 貓空纜車

Mass Rapid Transit (MRT) 捷運

meal n. 餐點

medium adj. 五分熟；半熟

message n. 訊息

metal n. 金屬

mind v.（用於否定句和疑問句中）介意；反對 +V-ing

mountain n. 山

museum n. 博物館

N

necessary adj. 必要的；必需的

network n. 網狀系統

newly adv. 新近；最近

noisy adj. 喧鬧的；嘈雜的

notify v. 通知；告知

O

ocean n. 海洋；海

offer v. 給予；提供

on time prep. phr. 準時

ordinary adj. 普通的

otherwise adv. 否則；不然

outside prep. 在外面；向外面

overseas adj. adv.（在）海外；（在）國外

overweight adj. 超重的；過重的

P

page v.（在公共場所）喊叫尋找；廣播叫（人）

Pardon me. 原諒我

park v. 停放（車）

party n.（共同工作或活動的）一團人；一夥人；一行人

passport n. 護照

passport number n. phr. 護照號碼

patience n. 耐心

payment n. 支付；付款

Pay-Per-View 收費的電視節目

photo n. 照片

pick up v. phr. 拾起；收拾

piece n. 一件

plastic adj. 塑膠的

pleasing adj. 令人愉快的；合意的；使人滿意的

pleasure n. 愉快；樂趣

poached adj. 水煮的

pocket n. 口袋

postage n. [U] 郵資；郵費

postal adj. 郵政的；郵件的

postcard n. 明信片

potential adj. 潛在的；可能的

prefer v. 更喜歡

prepare v. 準備；做（飯菜）；製作；調製

press v. 熨平（衣服）

private adj. 私人的

procedure n. 程序；手續；步驟

property n. 財產；資產；所有物

provide v. 提供

pub n. 酒吧

pull up v. phr.（使）停下來

purse n. 錢包；（女用）手提包

R

railway n. 鐵路；鐵道

rare adj. 生的

ready adj. 準備好的

receipt n. 收據

reception n. 接待；接受

receptionist n. 櫃台接務員

recommend v. 推薦；介紹

reconfirm v. 再證實；再確認；再確定

red wine n. phr. 紅酒

refill v. 再裝滿；再灌滿

registration n. 登記；註冊

remain v. 保持；仍是

replace v. 取代；以…代替

request n. v. 要求；請求

require v. 需要；要求

reserve v. 預訂

reserved adj. 留做專用的；預訂的

resident n. 居民；定居者

restaurant n. 餐廳

right adj. 正確的；準確的

room service n. phr. 客房服務

S

safe n. 保險箱

safe-deposit box n. 防火保險箱

safekeeping n. 保管處

sake n. 目的；理由

satisfactory adj.令人滿意的；符合要求的

scanner n. 掃描機

scenic adj. 風景的

schedule n. 時刻表；日程安排表

season n. 季節

seated adj. 就座的；有…座位的

selection n. 選擇

serve v. 供應(+with)；侍候（顧客等）；供應（飯菜）；端上

service n. 服務

service charge n. phr. 服務費

settle v. 支付；結算

shampoo n. 洗髮精

shape n. 形狀；情況；狀態

sharp adj. 鋒利的；尖的

shirt n. 襯衫

shot n.（烈酒等的）一口；一小杯

shower cap n. phr. 浴帽

shrink v. 收縮；縮短；皺縮（shrink-shrank-shrank）

shuttle bus n. phr. 接駁車

sightseeing n. 觀光；遊覽

signature n. 簽名

smoking area n. phr. 吸煙區

soap n. 肥皂

spill v. 使溢出；使濺出；使散落

spilt v. 濺（spill的過去式和過去分詞）

spot n. 地點

staff v. 給…配備職員

status n. 情形；狀況

stay n. 停留；逗留

still adj. 靜止的；不動的

store v. 保管；收存

subtropical adj. 副熱帶的

surround v. 圍；圍繞；圈住

sweater n. 毛線衣

swipe v. 碰擦；擦過

system n. 系統

T

tag n. 牌子；標籤

take a seat v. phr. 坐一下

Take your time 慢慢來

taxi n. 計程車

tea tasting n. phr. 飲茶

temperature n. 氣溫

terribly【口】adv. 很；非常

toiletries n. 盥洗用品

toll-free adj. 不用付電話費的

toothbrush n. 牙刷

toothpaste n. 牙膏

total adj. 總計的；總括的

traffic light n. phr 紅綠燈

transfer v. 轉接 be supposed to + 原形動詞 應該

transportation n. 運輸

travel agency n. phr. 旅行社

travel agent n. phr. 旅行社職員

tropical adj.熱帶的

turn in v. phr. 交上；歸還

typhoon n. 颱風

U

unique adj. 獨特的

usable adj. 可用的

vacancy n. 空桌；空房

V

valet n. 泊車人員

valuables n. 貴重物品；財產

value n. 價值；面額

view n. 景觀

visit v. 參觀

W

watch out for v. phr. 小心提防；注意

waiter n.（男）侍者；服務生

warmer n. 加熱器

watch out for v. phr. 小心提防；注意

weather forecast n. phr. 氣象預報

weatherman n. 氣象預報員

weigh v. 稱…的重量

well done adj. 全熟

What's going on? 發生了什麼事？

while conj. 而；然而

wonder v. 納悶；想知道

work v. 運作

wrong adj. 錯誤的

餐旅英文與會話

作　　者／謝雯雯
出 版 者／揚智文化事業股份有限公司
發 行 人／葉忠賢
總 編 輯／閻富萍
執行編輯／吳韻如
內頁插畫／黃威翔
地　　址／台北縣深坑鄉北深路三段 260 號 8 樓
電　　話／(02)8662-6826
傳　　真／(02)2664-7633
網　　址／http://www.ycrc.com.tw
 E-mail ／service@ycrc.com.tw
印　　刷／鼎易印刷事業股份有限公司
 I S B N ／978-957-818-962-1
初版一刷／2010 年 7 月
定　　價／新台幣 500 元

國家圖書館出版品預行編目資料

餐旅英文與會話＝Practical hotel, restaurant,
and travel English ／謝雯雯著. -- 初版. --
臺北縣深坑鄉：揚智文化，2010.07
　　面；　公分.
　　ISBN　978-957-818-962-1（平裝附光碟）

　　1.英語　2.旅遊　3.會話

805.188　　　　　　　　　　　　99010878